W9-AYB-778

"I think we need to ⟨⟩ behind us," Wyatt said.

"For Matty's sake."

Carolina's whole being, heart and soul, leaned into him, hoping beyond hope that there was something more.

He nodded slowly, never breaking eye contact with her. "Yes. For Matty."

Her heart dropped like lead.

"But," he continued, as a tumble of emotion squeezed the air out of her lungs, "not *just* Matty."

He reached for her, framing her face with one hand. They weren't the same people they had been three years ago. They had both changed. Matured.

They had a son now.

"Carolina, I—" He stopped abruptly.

She waited. Her capacity for speech had deserted her the moment Wyatt touched her.

* * *

Award-winning author **Deb Kastner** writes stories of faith, family and community in a small-town Western setting. Deb's books contain sigh-worthy heroes and strong heroines facing obstacles that draw them closer to each other and the Lord. She lives in Colorado with her husband and is blessed with three daughters and two grandchildren. She enjoys spoiling her grandkids, movies, music (The Texas Tenors!), singing in the church choir and exploring Colorado on horseback.

Visit the Author Profile page at Harlequin.com for more titles.

The Doctor's Texas Baby

Deb Kastner

HHARLEQUIN® LOVE INSPIRED®

Special thanks and acknowledgment are given to Deb Kastner for her contribution to the Lone Star Cowboy League: Boys Ranch miniseries.

Recycling programs for this product may not exist in your area.

LOVE INSPIRED BOOKS

ISBN-13: 978-0-373-89908-1

The Doctor's Texas Baby

www.Harlequin.com

Printed in U.S.A.

He has said,
"I will never forsake you or abandon you."
—*Hebrews* 13:5

To the Sacred Heart of Jesus.
May Your name ever be blessed.

Chapter One

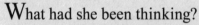

What had she been thinking?

There was no question in Carolina Mason's mind that returning to her hometown, Haven, Texas, was a bad idea.

Too many complications. Too many memories. Most of all, too much heartbreak.

And yet here she was. What few household goods she owned were now unpacked in her late great-uncle's cabin, where she'd made up a room for herself and one for her two-year-old son, Matty.

If she had any sense in this head of hers, she'd ignore all the rational reasons she'd come back to Haven in the first place, pack up her sedan again and go back from whence she'd come.

If there was a *back*.

Which there wasn't.

The truth was, she had ultimately returned to

Haven because, to her own shame and mortification, she had nowhere else to go.

She was facing a fairly insurmountable problem, as she saw it. No health, no home, no job and not much of an opportunity to get one. If it was just her life in the balance, she might have resisted the urge to return.

But this wasn't about her. It was about Matty. He needed the stability the small town offered, which she could not otherwise give him.

Uncle Mort's cabin was available to her rent-free. Where else would she find a deal like that? And though returning home wasn't exactly a typical fresh start, no other choices had presented themselves. She had to take what she could get.

Besides, she had important, possibly critical legal news to deliver to Bea Brewster, the director of the local boys ranch, information Carolina knew they were anxiously waiting on. The kind of news that was better delivered in person.

Since that was her first order of business after unloading all of her personal belongings, she headed to the boys ranch as soon as the moving truck had left her uncle's premises.

She paused at the door to the front office of the boys ranch and ran a palm down the denim of her jeans, considering her options for about the hundredth time that week. In one hand she clutched her purse, which contained the legal document the boys ranch director was awaiting. Matty clung tightly to her opposite arm, his hand squeezing hers.

He was usually an outgoing and curious toddler, but at the moment he was hiding behind Carolina and peeking out at his surroundings from around her leg.

Her heart clenched. She suspected her son's sudden shyness was due to his picking up on her nerves and anxiety. The poor child had had enough change, with his entire life being uprooted, without having the challenge of immediately adapting to his new surroundings.

"It's okay, little man. You and Mama are going to be just fine. You'll see." She affectionately and—she hoped—encouragingly ruffled his dark hair.

"Carolina!" Receptionist Katie Ellis exited through the front door of the office, a pink canvas lunch tote hanging from her elbow. "What a nice surprise!"

Any thoughts Carolina might have had of skipping town without being recognized dissipated into thin air as she nodded at her friend. Katie was a few years younger than Carolina but they had gotten to know each other while volunteering at community events and had become friends.

"It's good to see you," Carolina said, hoping the strain she was feeling didn't echo in her voice.

"Still working for the boys ranch, I see. It's been a long time."

"Too long," Katie agreed, racing forward to envelop Carolina in an enthusiastic hug. "How many years has it been, do you think?"

"Three." Carolina sighed inwardly, the ache in her chest growing. She knew *exactly* how long it had been since she'd last been in Haven. Not just to the year, but to the month. Even to the day.

Katie grasped Carolina's elbow and turned them both back toward her office.

"I don't want to interrupt your lunch hour," Carolina protested. "I can come back later."

"Nonsense." She held up her tote. "It's only a salad, and I'm heartily tired of eating greens every day. But wouldn't you know I have to perpetually diet just to keep my figure." She shrugged and grinned. "What's a single woman to do? Anyway, lunch will wait. I want to hear all about you. What's been happening in your life since you left Haven?"

Katie dropped into her chair behind the desk and gestured for Carolina to take a seat.

"I can see at least one thing has changed," Katie said with a giggle, gesturing at Matty.

Carolina tried to pull a wiggling Matty onto her lap, but he protested loudly and tried to squirm away.

"I'm sorry," she apologized to Katie. "I promise I'll fill you in, but I need to get Matty settled first."

She set him down on the floor by her feet and fished around in her oversize purse, triumphantly retrieving two toy cars. "Here you go, buddy. One for each fist. Stay close and play quietly, please."

Matty was already distracted, his attention on the little police car and fire truck he held in his hands.

Carolina returned her attention to Katie.

Katie leaned back in her seat and smiled. "Obviously you didn't have any trouble catching a man's eye, now did you? You look exactly the same as the day you left Haven. Or prettier, even. And you had a baby? Are you and your husband planning to move back to town with your sweet little boy?" Katie stopped hammering Carolina with questions long enough to give her a once-over. "I have to say I am seriously envious of your figure right now. How do you do it?"

Carolina bit back a bitter laugh. The compliment was sincere and well meant, but she was perfectly aware that the person who'd left Haven in such a rush three years ago was not even remotely the same as the woman who'd returned. She was older now, hopefully a little wiser, and infinitely worse for the wear.

Physically, emotionally and spiritually. If she

had kept her figure, it was because she was too stressed to eat most of the time.

Life had come full circle for her, and she was back in Haven, where she'd once found her deepest peace, her grandest love and her greatest heartbreak. She'd been pregnant and troubled when she'd left town.

The biggest change in her life was that she'd become a Christian while she'd been away, living in Colorado with a friend. She was still learning what her faith entailed. Trust didn't come easy to her, and thinking about God as a loving Father was still a concept she wrestled with. Her own father hadn't exactly been a good role model.

When she'd first escaped to Colorado and had no money to buy the food she'd needed to help her have a healthy pregnancy, folks from a nearby church had reached out to help her. They'd not only shared their food but their faith, and now it was Carolina's precarious trust in God's love and mercy that kept her going, knowing He held the future, even when from her perspective it was all jumbled up.

She prayed returning home was the right decision, that she would be able to recover some of the peace she'd once had.

But love?

That was so not happening. A romantic relationship was not even a blip on the radar, and she was fairly certain it never would be. She had her hands full raising Matty.

She tensed. This was the part she had dreaded and worried about the most in coming back to town.

Breathe in, breathe out.

It was no wonder Matty was picking up on her anxiety. It was practically radiating from her.

Presenting Matty to Katie and talking about him would be relatively easy compared to what she imagined it would be like with some of the other folks in town.

It was overwhelming to realize this was the first of many times she'd have to introduce her son—to friends and acquaintances, neighbors in town, and at church. And she'd have to explain that a husband didn't come along with the package.

She anticipated a few surprised looks, maybe even a little gossip, but hopefully no one would ask about the boy's father, at least not right away. She wasn't ready to open up about Matty's parentage, to disclose her secret.

Honestly, she doubted she'd ever be ready.

"No husband," she managed to choke out.

Katie's face turned a pretty shade of pink. "Oh, I'm sorry. I just assumed—"

Carolina sighed. "It's not a big deal. You had

no way of knowing. I'm sure you'll be the first of many to ask."

Actually, the question was like a jab in the stomach, but she knew she'd better get used to it.

"No worries there. Everyone is going to adore this handsome little fella," Katie assured her, clearly backtracking.

Carolina ran her palm across the cowlick in her son's dark hair, but he paid no attention to her as he busily pushed his cars across the tile floor, making vrooming and screeching noises, punctuated with the occasional fire truck or police vehicle siren.

Matty's resemblance to his father was striking, should anyone care to notice. Carolina prayed they wouldn't. If Katie didn't notice, maybe there was hope that others would miss the connection as well.

"Matty, be a gentleman and say hi to Miss Katie."

Hearing his name, Matty looked up from his toys.

"I'm Matty," he proclaimed proudly.

Katie chuckled. "Nice to meet you, Matty." Her gaze returned to Carolina, and her smile widened. "What a little sweetheart."

Carolina released the breath she hadn't even realized she'd been holding.

"Would you like to take a tour around our new

ranch? It's quite an improvement over the old one. Thanks to Cyrus Culpepper, we've been able to take in twice the number of needy boys."

"That's great news. What I saw driving in looks wonderful. Actually, I've got some important information about the Culpepper will. That's why I'm here." Carolina once again fished through her purse, this time searching for the certified letter she'd received the week previously.

She really did need to buy a smaller handbag that half of her worldly possessions wouldn't get lost in. After Matty had turned two, she'd graduated from a diaper bag to her current purse, which wasn't much smaller than the enormous blue elephant bag had been. But with an active toddler, she still found it necessary to carry a lot of stuff. Toy cars, a pull-on diaper or two, wet wipes, fruit snacks…

Finally locating and retrieving the envelope, she placed it on the desk in front of her. "I need to speak to Bea. I believe it's regarding a legal matter."

"Of course. She's out to lunch right now, but I expect her back in a half an hour or so. I'll text her to let her know you're here."

Carolina shifted her gaze to Matty just as, standing on tiptoe, he reached for the stack of papers teetering on the edge of Katie's desk.

"Matty, no," Carolina barked, just barely managing to snatch him out of the way before the whole stack of invoices went flying off the desk. As it was, four or five documents fluttered to the ground around her feet.

Shaking her head in dismay, she propped Matty on her hip and turned to Katie. "I'm so sorry. Sometimes I think curiosity should have been Matty's middle name."

Heat suffused Carolina's face. She only hoped Katie would not ask what Matty's real middle name was. It would be a dead giveaway for sure.

Katie grinned and stood, moving around the desk and stooping to retrieve the errant papers. "Not a problem. No harm done."

Carolina returned her smile. "Yet. This child can get into mischief faster than you can say Jack Frost. I'm his mother and I can barely keep up with him."

"Do you like horses, Matty? I think we have just enough time before Miss Bea gets back for us to go visit the stables." She winked at Carolina. "And get him out for some fresh air? Maybe run off a bit of his energy? If only we could bottle it up and use it for ourselves, huh?" she said. "Imagine how much we could accomplish in a day."

Carolina laughed and nodded. "I'll say."

As Katie led them between outbuildings toward the stable, she regaled Carolina with funny stories about the resident boys and the animals and pointed out various buildings and working areas of the boys ranch.

Carolina was familiar with the general purpose of the ranch, which, under the guidance of the Lone Star Cowboy League, was to care for and mentor troubled boys ages six to seventeen, kids who were having difficulties at home. Most of the time their parents or caregivers, unable to deal with the boys' emotional issues on their own, placed them at the boys ranch for a time. These were the kids who were walking a fine line, and the ranch had many success stories of kids who had grown up and gone on to be model citizens and useful members of their communities.

Since Carolina wasn't personally connected to the ranch in any way, she knew very little about the specifics and had never visited. Three years ago when she'd left Haven, it had still been located at the smaller facility, which had only had the capacity to house twelve boys. Now that they'd moved, they'd been able to expand the children's options and aid them in moving forward with their lives.

As Katie talked, Carolina became increasingly impressed by the number of programs the ranch now offered to help the boys transition into public life, to become honorable, faithful and hardworking members of society. They attended the nearby public school during the week and Haven Community Church on Sundays.

The boys also had the opportunity to acquire a trade. In addition to ranch work, they could learn cooking, carpentry, welding, painting, plumbing—the impressive list went on and on.

Carolina took a deep breath of the country air and reveled in the uniquely rural aroma that assaulted her nostrils—the pungent odors of hay and horses, prairie grass, and freshly dug earth mingled with the scents of the barnyard animals they passed. Oddly, it wasn't an unpleasant sensation. After three years in the city, the ranch smelled like home.

White picket fences surrounded the property. Brown cattle dotted the rolling green hills. Matty was entranced by the squawking chickens pecking for food on the ground inside their coop. Carolina chuckled at the plump piglets rooting around in the mud, grunting to their hearts' content.

Her ears picked up on the congregational sound of bleating. A herd of hungry sheep, perhaps. Or goats.

She wondered if they might be able to take a quick detour to introduce Matty to the goats. Her son would go crazy over a cute little bleating baby with its nubby horns and curious nature. What were they called again?

Kids?

Carolina chuckled. That sounded about right, given that goats were similarly stubborn and inclined to get themselves into loads of mischief.

"I'm really excited about one of our newest projects," Katie gushed as they rounded the corner of the barn. "It's already proving to be one of the most popular programs we've ever had here on the ranch."

Carolina pulled her cell phone from her back pocket and checked the time, thinking that, although she hated to cut the visit short, she should probably suggest returning to the office so she could be waiting there to speak to Bea when the director returned from her lunch.

As much as she was enjoying the tour of the ranch, and especially watching Matty interact with the animals, it was more imperative than ever that she speak to the ranch's director as soon as possible. She'd had no idea of the length and breadth of the boys ranch activities, and now that she knew more about it, she realized just how important her information was.

It broke her heart that she was the bearer of bad news that could possibly affect the ranch's future. Hopefully not, but the sooner they got the information, the better. Her great-uncle Morton, whom the lawyer representing the ranch was seeking, had recently died of a heart attack.

A moment's grief swirled through her and she swallowed hard. She'd been especially close to her great-uncle, and his passing had been hard on her. Gritting her teeth, she stared at her boots as she mentally herded her emotions into the deepest corner of her heart and clamped them down with the strength of her will.

"Katie, I should probably—"

Blinking back tears, she looked up to find a man's dark eyes on hers. Their eyes met and locked, surprise and shock registering within his deep stare.

She gasped, her entire body stiffening like a slab of concrete.

He swallowed hard enough to make his Adam's apple bob. Clearly he was every bit as stunned as she was.

Oh, no. No, no, no, no, no.

This couldn't be happening.

Wyatt Harrow.

The man who'd won her heart and then shattered it into a million pieces.

No—that wasn't fair to him. She couldn't honestly place the blame at his door for what had happened. Not when she was the one at fault—for everything.

For not knowing better than to trust her own heart. For not having the strength to stay in control of her emotions enough not to surrender to the physical need to find comfort for their mutual grief. For not being brave enough to tell Wyatt the truth about Matty, even if she'd believed— and still believed—that it was in his best interest not to know.

She'd been the one to abruptly end their relationship, not Wyatt. She'd literally walked away from him, and from Haven, even though her heart had been breaking into smaller and smaller pieces with every step she took, for every mile of distance she put between them.

His presence was like a slap on the face.

Wyatt was here. He'd seen her. There was no turning away now. Nowhere to run or hide from the truth.

She felt as if she were drowning. She coaxed herself to breathe through the crashing waves of reality, but the air seemed to freeze in her lungs as she watched him slowly recover from his own shock.

Surrounded by a herd of goats and a motley flock of boys displaying varying degrees of interest in what he was doing, Wyatt was clearly in the middle of some kind of veterinary demonstration. He had a syringe in one hand and a goat trapped between his muscular legs.

He was every bit as handsome and rugged as she remembered, from the tip of his black Stetson to the toes of his tan cowboy boots. Jet-black hair, eyes the color of dark chocolate, powerful biceps, broad shoulders sloping to a cowboy's trim waist. A well-worn T-shirt that might once have been red, a fleece-lined denim jacket and tattered jeans that spoke of his hard manual labor as a large-animal veterinarian.

The only thing that had changed from the last time she had seen him, from the man she had left three years ago, were the lines of strain on his face and the pure icy coldness of his gaze. Her heart clenched as she remembered how his eyes used to warm when he looked at her, when his whole countenance lit up whenever she was around.

But not now.

He pulled his hat down to shadow his thoughts, but he couldn't hide the frown that curved his lips into a downward arch.

What was Wyatt doing here?

Not just here at the boys ranch. That much was fairly evident.

But why was he still in Haven?

Carolina quivered from the adrenaline still coursing through her. It hadn't even occurred to her that she might run into him. She had been so certain he would be long gone from town by now, or else she would never have even considered returning—letter or no letter.

That was the whole point, wasn't it? Why she'd left in the first place? To give Wyatt his freedom?

Wyatt stood to his full height, and Carolina's breath snagged in her throat. She'd hoped that if she ever saw him again she would feel nothing, that she would have moved beyond the long nights and emotions born of grief and loneliness.

Instead, nothing had changed, except perhaps that her feelings had grown stronger over time. It was as if every nerve in her body was attuned to his.

The brown-speckled goat Wyatt had been working on bleated and bolted away, but he didn't appear to notice. His posture was stiff and intimidating as he stared back at her, tight jawed and frowning.

"Carolina." His usually rich baritone emerged low and gritty.

"Mama?" Matty squeezed her hand.

She'd been so shocked by Wyatt's sudden appearance that she'd momentarily forgotten Matty was at her side.

Wyatt's gaze shifted to Matty and then back up to her again, his eyes widening in surprise.

Now the electricity intensified, zapping back and forth like lightning between them. Her pulse ratcheted. Her heart hammered. Her worst fear, realized.

Matty.

Oh, precious Lord, please help me.

Even as she prayed for relief, she knew there was no way out of this. It didn't matter that she hadn't intended to reveal this secret. Not to anyone, but most especially not to Wyatt.

Ever.

The whole reason she'd left Haven was to allow Wyatt to pursue the life he'd dreamed of. Ever since she'd known him, he'd spoken about his desire to help the poor and destitute in foreign countries learn how to raise animals. He wanted to provide them with a trade through which they could work themselves out of a poverty-stricken existence.

It was a noble goal, the dream of his heart, and if she had stayed, she would have ruined it for him. His parents had been foreign diplomats who'd died in an explosion, and Wyatt had never quite gotten over the loss, even if it made him more determined than ever to help those less fortunate than him. She'd known him well enough to know there was no way he would ever consider bringing a wife and child with him to a third-world country where they might be in danger.

Carolina had known and understood this, and she'd loved him enough to let him go. That was why she'd left Haven so suddenly when she'd discovered she was pregnant with Matty. Everything she'd been through since then—every struggle, every trial she'd endured, every night spent crying in her pillow, had been for Wyatt's sake.

Because if he'd known she was pregnant, he would have had no choice but to stay with her in Haven. He wasn't the kind of man who would walk away from his responsibilities. He would have given up all of his personal hopes and dreams for the sake of his son. She had no doubt whatsoever that he was the guy who would do the right thing by her and by Matty. He would have asked her to marry him.

But she'd been in love with him, and the *right thing* wasn't good enough for her—or for Matty. Their lives couldn't be built on one night's mistake.

If she'd believed Wyatt was in love with her, that would have been one thing. But before the night Matty was conceived they'd only been casually dating, and the night they'd shared had been born of sorrow, not joy. A marriage and family based only on a man's sense of decency and not true love? Her heart couldn't take it.

So she'd left.

And now she was back, only to discover Wyatt had never left at all. Why wasn't he in Uganda or deep in the Amazon jungle somewhere?

Had her sacrifice been for nothing?

"Mama?" Matty said again, yanking her arm more intently this time. "Mama. Mama."

She scooped him into her arms and gently patted his back, reassuring herself as much as him. Her fight-or-flight instinct was working overtime, and it was all she could do to stand firm and not flee.

But what good would it do her to turn away now? Wyatt had already caught sight of Matty. He was watching the toddler through narrowed eyes and pressed lips as the boy tangled his fingers into Carolina's hair.

"You're a mama?" Wyatt asked, and for one confused moment, no longer than a blink of an eye, Carolina thought…hoped…*prayed* that he wouldn't comprehend what that meant. That he wouldn't realize the truth about those identical chocolate-brown eyes that were literally staring right back at him, among the many features that mirrored his own.

"I—how could you?" he stammered, picking off his hat and threading his fingers through his hair.

Carolina cringed, waiting for him to come loose at the seams. How could he not? She wouldn't blame him. He had every right to be furious.

She held her breath, waiting for the explosion she knew was coming.

But when he spoke, it was deep, and hushed, and as hard and cold as steel.

"Tell me the truth, Carolina, for once in your life. This boy—is he my son?"

Wyatt's breath felt like icicles in his lungs, poking and puncturing his chest with each ragged gasp.

That boy, the animated, dark-haired, dark-eyed child clinging to Carolina's neck, was his *son*.

For the very first few seconds after he'd realized Carolina wasn't alone, that she had her toddler with her, there had been a flash of confusion—of anger, of *envy*—that she had been able to move on with her life so quickly after abandoning him. It had taken him months to recover enough to go on with his daily life without thinking of her with every heartbeat, and there were still days—and nights—he found difficulty putting the past behind him.

And she already had a husband and a toddler? She must have met the guy right after—

His gaze had dropped to her left hand, but her ring finger was bare. So she wasn't married, then.

Yet there was a child.

And then, in an instant, it all came together.

The moment he looked into the child's eyes, Wyatt *knew*, with the same certainty that he recognized the wild, unsteady rhythm of his heart beating in his chest, that the little boy was his son.

His child.

He didn't have to count back the months or measure the years. Anyone with eyes could see the resemblance.

The boy could have stepped right out of a photograph of Wyatt at that age, from the stubborn cowlick in his black hair right down to the curve of his dimples when he smiled. Wyatt now covered his dimples with a few days' growth of beard, but they were there. Just like this boy's.

"What's his name?" he ground out, barely able to find his voice.

"Matty," Carolina answered shakily.

Matty was his son.

His thoughts were coming quick and choppy, echoing over and over in his mind, each time stronger and with increasing clarity.

Matty was his own flesh and blood, created out of his love for Carolina. They'd done everything backward, to be sure, but even before Matty had been conceived, Wyatt had had every intention of asking Carolina to marry him, had been ready to make a lifetime commitment to her.

Obviously Carolina hadn't felt the same way about him, or else she never would have left him.

Left. Knowing she was keeping him from his son.

Where was the love in that?

The little boy staring back at him with wide, curious brown eyes should have had the benefit of his father's love and attention from the very day he was born.

Already those emotions were welling in Wyatt's heart. One second ago he'd been a single man. Now he was a daddy.

The whole scenario was wrong on so many levels. He should have been there when Matty was born. When he took his first steps. Said his first word. Wyatt would have showered Matty with love and attention. He and Matty had both been cheated out of time together.

Years.

For a reason Wyatt couldn't begin to comprehend, Carolina had willingly chosen to live as a single mother, without so much as asking him for financial support, much less anything emotional.

His gut fisted as another thought occurred to him.

Was there another man in the picture now? The fact that Carolina wasn't wearing a wedding band didn't necessarily mean anything. The woman he'd thought he'd known would never live with another man without being married to him, but what did he really know about her?

She had proven him wrong in every way that mattered.

Had Wyatt been replaced before he'd ever even had the opportunity to be a dad to his son? The idea of someone else taking on his role of father to Matty made him sick.

It was too much information to process, too many emotions to contain all at once.

Bewilderment, uncertainty, grief, pain, fury—yet at the same time an affection and warmth unlike any he'd ever known. He had no idea where the tender feelings for Matty came from. They were just *there*.

He switched his gaze to Carolina. She looked stricken, as well she might.

How dare she keep all knowledge of his son from him for all this time?

And why had she come back now?

He guessed the boy had to be around two years of age. Had Carolina suddenly grown a conscience and decided Wyatt needed to know about the boy? It didn't seem likely, especially since Carolina appeared completely shocked to have encountered him the way she had. She certainly hadn't been seeking him out.

There were so many questions he wanted answered, so much confusion rolling through his mind and heart that he couldn't seem to form the words to voice a single one of them. He wanted to grill and interrogate Carolina on every aspect of Matty's life, but he didn't know where to begin.

And really, what did it matter anyway?

The fact was, three years ago Carolina had left

him high and dry with no notice and no explanation, and now, years later, she had suddenly returned with *their* son in her arms.

He couldn't imagine any conceivable excuse or reasonable explanation that he would actually accept as a legitimate reason why she hadn't bothered to tell him about his child. There was simply nothing she could say to talk her way out of the conversation they were about to have.

"W-Wyatt?" Seventeen-year-old Johnny Drake touched his shoulder and tentatively broke into his thoughts. The teenager, whom Wyatt was personally mentoring, was reed thin, with floppy, curly brown hair and clothes that always looked like they were a size too large for him. "D-did you want me to c-catch the g-g-goat for you?"

In the shock of finding out he had a son, Wyatt had completely forgotten he was in the middle of teaching a class to a rowdy group of boys who were all gazing at him with wide-eyed curiosity and far more attention than they'd been giving him when he'd been explaining how to inoculate a goat.

"Yeah, W-W-Wyatt," said Christopher Harrington, a resentful young man who thought he was better than the others because he came from a wealthy home. Christopher hadn't yet learned the hard truth that the boys were all on equal footing here at the ranch. "What about the g-g-g-g-g-goats?"

Wyatt frowned at Christopher's exaggerated stutter as he made fun of Johnny. Poor Johnny's shoulders drooped and his bitter gaze sizzled the ground at his feet.

"Knock it off, Christopher. You boys are done for the day. Go somewhere else and find something useful to do."

The young men didn't have to be told twice before they scattered. They weren't used to receiving a sudden chunk of free time.

Only Johnny hung back and didn't follow the other boys. His stutter made him the object of ridicule, but Johnny found solace reading books and working with the ranch animals, who accepted him just the way he was.

Wyatt understood that, which was one of the main reasons he had taken Johnny under his wing, mentoring the boy with an eye to getting him into college and eventually, if Johnny excelled in his studies, veterinary school.

As much as the teenagers mercilessly teased Johnny, that was nothing close to what would happen if they got a whiff of what was happening between Wyatt and Carolina now. There was no telling what kind of havoc the boys would wreak with that kind of information.

It was time to be proactive, to deal with this

situation with Carolina and Matty before anyone else found out about what had happened between them. They needed to get their stories straight and nip any rumors in the bud.

Or did everyone already know?

Was it possible that he was the only man in Haven who wasn't aware he had a son?

Fury and humiliation lapped like flames in his chest and he struggled to maintain his composure. He gritted his teeth and crossed his arms, digging his fingernails into his biceps and fighting for control of his temper.

"I know you must be angry with me." Carolina paused, her eyes uncertain. "Aren't you?"

He raised his eyebrows.

Angry?

That was the understatement of the century. He was mad enough to want to put his fist through a brick wall, just to try to transfer some of the pain in his chest to his hand. He felt like he was about to explode.

"How long were you planning on keeping this secret from me?" he snapped, jamming his hands into the pockets of his fleece-lined jeans jacket to keep from punching the air in frustration. "I can't believe you kept my own *son* from me, Carolina. How could you?"

"I never meant to hurt you."

The fire in his chest burned even hotter. How

could she even consider suggesting that her motives were altruistic? Did she really think that leaving him without sharing the knowledge that she was carrying his baby wouldn't wound him?

He scoffed. "Of course not. You somehow thought I'd be better off not knowing that I have a son."

"W-W-Wyatt?"

Wyatt turned. He'd somehow forgotten—again—that Johnny was still at his side.

The boy pushed his hair off his forehead. Wyatt could see how agitated Johnny was, clenching and unclenching his fists in a silent, steady rhythm. The poor kid looked like he was about to jump out of his skin.

It struck Wyatt suddenly that *he* was the cause. Johnny was ultrasensitive and was picking up on the tension between him and Carolina. Wyatt took a deep breath and let it out slowly. No sense upsetting the young man. There was enough anger and grief in this scenario without involving the boy.

He clapped a hand on Johnny's shoulder. "Don't worry. It's all good. Carolina and I just have a few…issues to work out between us."

He pointed to the herd of goats, who were now grazing their way through another field. "Do you think you could finish vaccinating the goats?"

Wyatt nodded toward the clipboard, which contained the list of the names of all the goats. He'd dropped the clipboard in the grass earlier, when he'd had his hands full teaching the group of boys how to give a goat a subcutaneous vaccine.

"I think there are four or five of them we haven't vaccinated yet. Do you remember how to do it?"

"Y-y-yes, sir," replied Johnny, looking relieved to have a reason to avoid being around the strained reunion between Wyatt and Carolina.

Wyatt returned his attention to Carolina and Matty, who was now wiggling and squirming in his mother's arms, pumping his chunky arms and legs in an awkward rhythm. He clearly wanted to get down, but Carolina refused, clutching the child like a lifeline.

Wyatt clenched his fists. Had his heated response affected Matty as it had Johnny?

With every ounce of his self-control, Wyatt pressed his anger—along with all of his other barely containable and ignitable emotions—to the back of his mind and heart and firmly boarded them in.

He had to get past the fact that Carolina had abruptly sprung fatherhood on him. All that mattered was taking care of Matty. His needs would always come first, no matter what.

Wyatt was going to be there for his son, and that started right now.

"Can I—" he fumbled, but his voice was husky. He cleared his throat. "May I hold him?"

"Of course." Carolina sounded surprised that he would ask—as if she hadn't expected him to step up to the plate.

What was she thinking? That he would deny the truth that was right in front of his eyes? Or maybe it was the opposite—that she feared he was going to step in and take over.

Now *that* was a thought.

He held out his arms to Matty, feeling suddenly large and ungainly. Abruptly shy, Matty tucked his head into his mother's shoulder and curled closer to her.

Wyatt's heart plummeted and he dropped his hands to his sides, wiping his sweaty palms against the denim of his blue jeans.

Strike one.

"Wyatt, wait." Carolina held up her hand to him, gesturing for him to come closer. Then to Matty, she said, "Son, this is—" She stopped abruptly, her eyes widening in dismay as it met Wyatt's. "Um—this is Mr. Wyatt. He's a very nice man. Don't you want to say hello to him?"

Mr. Wyatt. Not Father. Not Daddy.

Talk about disheartening. But then, what did he expect from his first encounter with his son? That the years apart didn't matter? That Matty didn't know him from a stranger?

He *was* a stranger to his son.

He stuffed the anger down as quickly as it rose, afraid Matty would be able to sense it.

At least this time, when Wyatt reached for him, Matty stretched out his little arms and wrapped them tightly around Wyatt's neck.

Wyatt struggled to swallow, and not because Matty was cutting off his air. It just felt so new. So strange.

And yet somehow, so *right*.

Matty still sported the chunky arms and legs and chubby cheeks of toddlerhood, so Wyatt was surprised by how light the boy was. Wasn't he getting enough to eat?

"Where are you staying?" he asked as he mentally adjusted to the feel of Matty in his arms. He wasn't accustomed to holding children of any age. He was much more comfortable around the animals he vetted. He was only just getting used to teaching the kids at the boys ranch, and there wasn't much physical contact between them, other than the occasional encouraging pat on the back.

And all of the sudden he had a two-year-old son?

"We're lodging at my great-uncle's cabin for now," Carolina answered. An emotion Wyatt couldn't interpret flashed across her face.

For now.

What did that mean? That she wasn't planning to stick around?

Surely not. She couldn't be so coldhearted as to just waltz into town, inform Wyatt that he had a son and then disappear again.

Could she?

He didn't have the opportunity to clarify, because at that moment Bea Brewster approached, saying she'd managed to round up Gabe Everett, who was the president of the local chapter of the Lone Star Cowboy League, and attorney Harold Haverman, who was representing the Culpepper estate. They were awaiting Carolina's presence in Bea's office.

Carolina reached for Matty, and Wyatt reluctantly handed him back to her. Right when he was starting to adjust to the feel of Matty's chubby little body in his arms, the boy had been taken from him. Wyatt desperately craved more time. Much more.

He started to follow Carolina to Bea's office but then paused. If Gabe and a lawyer were involved in the meeting, it wasn't exactly his business to invite himself. Though he didn't know any of the details, he assumed the gathering had something to do with the terms of Cyrus Culpepper's will and the town's ability to retain the new boys ranch facility.

Before Carolina went anywhere, though, Wyatt

intended to tell her where he stood in regard to fatherhood—in regard to Matty. He wanted to make sure his feelings on the matter were perfectly clear.

He just needed the opportunity, which would be difficult when Carolina was deep in conversation with Bea.

"You are welcome to join us, Wyatt," Bea offered, casting a grin at him.

Wyatt agreed right away, partially because he volunteered at the boys ranch and thus had some vested interest in the legal matters that would be presented, but mostly because he was determined to find the opportunity to speak to Carolina once the meeting was adjourned.

As they walked back toward Bea's office, Wyatt gave Bea an apologetic smile and snagged Carolina's elbow, urging her aside for a moment. He bent his head to whisper close to her ear so the others wouldn't hear.

Her eyes met his, large and unblinking. He'd forgotten the way those pretty golden-brown eyes, rimmed with thick, dark lashes, used to do a number on him.

Well, not this time. He ignored the tightening of his throat and the way his gut flipped over.

"We're not finished here," he warned.

"No. I didn't think we were." Her gaze broke away from his and she sighed deeply.

"Just so I know we're on the same page." His voice was low and huskier than usual.

The same *page*?

They weren't even in the same *bookstore*. The three previous years spanned behind them like a dilapidated rope bridge, and an enormous, gaping breach lay before them. From his vantage point, it seemed like an impossible chasm to cross.

But he had to try.

For his son.

For Matty.

Carolina felt very much like she'd just escaped a firing squad, if only temporarily.

How had she not planned for this contingency? Why had it not occurred to her that, free from the burden she and Matty would have been for him, Wyatt would not have taken the very first plane out of the country?

But she hadn't, and Wyatt was here in Haven, and she didn't know what she was going to do about it.

She didn't even know what her options were.

Maybe she should just take care of this legal matter and leave Haven behind her, this time for good.

Except, she reminded herself, she had nowhere else to go. No family. No friends outside Haven other than her ex-roommate and work acquaintances. Nothing.

She'd been living in Colorado since she'd left Haven, working as a nurse at a senior center and hospice. She was surviving, if not thriving, as a single mother. She'd found the Lord, and God was faithfully seeing her through, one deliberate step at a time.

But then, in a matter of weeks, her life had completely upended and fallen apart. She'd taken a bad turn on a ski slope and trashed her knee, which had required major surgery and months of physical therapy. And then her great-uncle Mort had passed away.

Between her hospital stay and recovery, combined with her doctor permanently banning her from lifting more than fifty pounds, her entire life had quickly fallen apart at the seams. Lifting fifty pounds—sometimes much more when patients slipped and fell—was required for a first responder in a nursing home, and the senior center had simply let her go, which was a nice, polite way of saying she was fired.

And then, to top it all off, her roommate, who had been Matty's primary caretaker while Carolina was in the hospital, had eloped with her boyfriend, leaving Carolina on her own without the means to cover her month-to-month rent on her apartment and nobody available to watch her son while she looked for work.

It was a catch-22 to put all others to shame.

It had frightened her beyond measure that there was a very real possibility that she and Matty might end up living in a homeless shelter. She might have grown up in the country with a single mother, where there was sometimes little left over, but there had always been a roof over her head and enough food to go around.

Now it was her responsibility to make sure Matty had the same security.

Somehow.

As devastated as she'd been about Uncle Mort's passing, when she discovered he had willed her his cabin in Haven, it had been an answer to her prayer. Owning his cabin free and clear, she would be able to live rent-free—at least until she got back on her feet and was more financially stable. Then she could make more permanent decisions about their future.

The letter from Haven's Lone Star Cowboy League arrived soon after, when she was packing up her apartment to make the move, and she felt as if the Lord was validating and confirming her plans. After the frightening time when it had felt like her whole life was going down the drain, life suddenly appeared to be on an uptick.

She thought maybe everything might be turning around, falling into place for her and Matty.

And they had been.

Until she'd run smack-dab into Wyatt. Now she was wondering if her life had just taken the biggest downturn of all.

"Carolina," Bea said, her voice breaking sharply into Carolina's thoughts. With effort, she turned her attention to Bea. "First, we would all like to express our appreciation for your rapid response to our letter." Bea took a seat behind her desk and clasped her hands in front of her, her expression unusually grim. "And we appreciate the fact that you've taken the time out of your busy schedule to come see us."

Carolina bit the inside of her lip. If only Bea knew. Her schedule was, unfortunately, wide-open.

"We were concerned when we never heard directly from Morton," Bea continued politely.

Bea was a tall middle-aged woman with bobbed brown hair and dark eyes set off by horn-rimmed glasses. She definitely looked the part of the capable boys ranch director—which was the position she'd maintained for approximately the last twenty years. Her sensible jeans and well-worn boots attested to her proficiency.

Carolina was acquainted with Gabe, a muscular, dark-haired man with friendly blue eyes. He'd been a couple of years ahead of her in school. She assumed that the imposing silver-haired man who popped his leather briefcase open on the corner of Bea's desk was Harold Haverman, the lawyer representing the Culpepper estate.

Even though Wyatt hung back, leaning his broad shoulder against the door frame instead of fully entering the office, Carolina felt his presence so deeply that it filled the entire room.

Or maybe it was her own tension burdening her. Sadly, she did not come bearing good news.

Wyatt moved out of the doorway in order for Katie to enter.

"Did you want me to take care of Matty while y'all are talking?" she asked with a friendly smile.

"I would appreciate that," said Carolina, relieved not to have to worry about her loud, wiggly toddler while she worked out some of her other issues. It was going to be hard enough to get through these next few minutes without having a curious little boy trying to get into everything that wasn't tied down. "Thank you so much."

Katie held out her hand to Matty and he took it without a fuss.

"Not a problem," Katie replied brightly before turning her attention to Matty. "As I recall, we never quite made it to the stable earlier. What do you say, Matty? Do you want to come with me and see some real live horsies?"

Matty squealed in delight and everyone chuckled along with him, even Carolina. The little boy's laughter was definitely contagious.

But as soon as Katie and Matty left the room, the heaviness Carolina had earlier felt in the air reappeared. Everyone instantly became serious as all attention turned to the legal matter at hand.

Carolina let out a deep, shaky breath. No matter how many times she had rehearsed it in her head, she still couldn't say the words without trembling.

"I'm sorry I don't have better news for you. The reason you never heard from my uncle Mort is that—that is—" She cleared her throat and hiccuped a breath, struggling to finish her statement. "Unfortunately, my great-uncle passed away a month ago."

A widower, Morton had remarried at the age of seventy-five and moved in with his new wife's family in Amarillo, leaving his cabin in Haven unoccupied for a couple of years.

Compassion filled Bea's eyes. "Oh, I'm so sorry to hear that, my dear. We didn't know. My deepest condolences."

Carolina's throat grew tight and tears burned the backs of her eyes. She'd known coming into the meeting that this was going to be difficult for her to talk about, with her own grief still so fresh, but with all the added emotions brought on by encountering Wyatt, her sorrow was almost more than she could bear.

"Thank you," she scraped out, tears making a slow line down her cheeks. "He died in his sleep. His wife said it was peaceful. I—m-miss him," she stammered.

"Of course you do," said Bea. "Poor darling."

The office suddenly felt twenty degrees warmer and all the oxygen seemed to have been sucked out of the room. Her head spun and she clutched her throat, wavering.

Carolina blinked rapidly, trying to regain her equilibrium, but it felt as if she were in a narrow tunnel and darkness was edging out the light.

She gasped for breath and held out her arm, grateful when she felt a stabilizing hand at the small of her back. It was only when he pressed a handkerchief into her hand that she realized it was Wyatt by her side, silently urging her into the only other chair in the room.

She couldn't speak or even compose a smile, but she nodded her appreciation.

His eyes widened and his worried frown hardened to rigid planes, his dark eyebrows dropping low and his lips pressing into a firm, straight line. His eyes appeared almost as black as his hair.

Her heart took a wild ride, leaping into her throat and then plunging back down again to lodge uncomfortably in her sour stomach.

Three years hadn't changed Wyatt. Not where it really counted. He was ever the gentleman, even when it went against his own better judgment. He'd taken care of her even when he was beyond furious with her, which he had every right to be. After all that had been said and done, no matter what had happened between them, he hadn't let her fall.

The attorney cleared his throat. "I don't want to sound insensitive here, but we need to address the issue of the will and Morton's part in it. Cyrus specifically indicated that all four original members of the boys ranch had to be present at the seventieth-anniversary party or the land will be forfeited."

Gabe frowned and tapped his Stetson against his thigh. "This new development certainly throws another wrench in our plans."

Another wrench? Carolina wondered what other complications they'd already encountered, but she was still too shaken up to be able to formulate any questions.

Bea steepled her fingers under her chin, clearly deep in thought. "So what do we do now, Harold? Can you tell us if Cyrus considered any such contingencies, or should we just call a halt to this whole investigation? We've already put so much effort into finding the original men that it would be a real shame if we have to end it so abruptly.

Frankly, I'm terrified that we may have jumped the gun in taking on twelve extra boys, no matter how desperate the need may have been. I don't know what we're going to do if we have to give up this ranch after all we've done to expand the program. It just breaks my heart to even think about it."

Harold riffled through the files in his briefcase, at length removing one that contained several manila envelopes. He flipped through them and withdrew one near the bottom.

"Ah. Here we are."

Carolina's breath caught as she waited, although she didn't know for what. She felt nauseated. She hadn't realized in coming here that she wasn't just delivering the awful news of her great-uncle's passing, but apparently, she'd just put the final torch to the plans to expand the boys ranch. She'd assumed, when she'd read the letter requesting her great-uncle's presence in Haven for the anniversary party, that informing Bea and the other leaders of the boys ranch about Uncle Mort's death would simply put an end to any obligation he might have had in the matter. She'd never dreamed this information would create what now appeared to be an insurmountable difficulty to the whole process.

Harold picked up a letter opener from his briefcase, made a neat slice across the top of the manila envelope and then pulled out a single sheet of paper. He leaned his hip against the side of the desk and shook the paper to open it fully.

"I was instructed to open and read this letter in the case of this particular—er—contingency," he said, flashing Carolina an apologetic look. "It's addressed to next of kin. Would you like to read it, Carolina?"

Carolina shook her head. She couldn't yet find her voice, much less control her emotions. "No, thank you. This letter involves everyone here. Please read it to all of us."

Harold nodded gravely. "Of course."

He cleared his throat and began.

I, Cyrus B. Culpepper, being of sound mind and in front of witnesses, add this addendum to my will. It occurs to me that one or the other of the four fellows I'm requiring to be at the seventieth-anniversary party might have gone to meet their maker even before I do. Should you discover that to be the case, then I hereby declare that the next of kin may represent the family legacy at the celebration, assuming the next of kin is willing to attend the party.

Yours,

Cyrus B. Culpepper

Silence shrouded the room as each person ruminated over the new contingency. Then all eyes lifted and turned expectantly to Carolina. Would she stay and represent the Mason family?

"The next of kin would be Morton's wife, yes?" Bea asked.

Carolina shook her head. "Unfortunately, my aunt Martha died just a few weeks after Morton. Since my parents have also both passed away, I believe I am all that's left of Uncle Morton's legacy."

She didn't know whether to be relieved or alarmed.

On one hand, she was pleased that she would be able to help keep the boys ranch going and that she hadn't been delivering a literal death blow.

On the other hand, that meant she had to stay in Haven. It was the beginning of February, which meant she was looking at two months, before the party in March. If things went downhill between her and Wyatt, which well they might, she wouldn't have the option to pack up and be on the next bus out of town, away from Haven and away from Wyatt, for good.

As tempting as the idea was of cutting out of town without having to deal with Wyatt at all, there was no question about her staying. Not really.

It wasn't enough that she didn't have anywhere

else to go. She couldn't leave the boys ranch in the lurch. She simply couldn't. It meant too much to too many people, especially all the boys it had helped over the years—and would assist in the future, especially if they were able to keep the larger facility.

Seventy years of helping young men find a better way. She couldn't put her own needs and desires over something as amazing as that.

But more than that, when she stopped to truly examine her feelings, she knew in her heart that she couldn't leave without allowing Wyatt to get to know his son. Merely thinking about staying was more frightening than anything else she'd ever experienced—even reluctantly coming to the decision to leave town alone and pregnant three years ago.

She would have to own up to her choices. All of them, both good and bad.

She'd realized as soon as she'd seen the brokenhearted look on Wyatt's face that she'd been wrong to keep Matty's existence a secret from him. Matty was as much his son as he was hers.

He deserved to know his child. And now he would.

In a way God had made the decision for her, which was probably good, because her record in the decision-making department was deplorable of late.

She had to stay. So she would give Wyatt these two months to get to know Matty, to spend time with him and possibly build a bond as father and son. After that, only the Lord knew what would happen.

She came out of her thoughts to realize the others in Bea's office were still waiting for her answer. She took a deep, cleansing breath and dived in without knowing just how deep the water was.

"Okay. I'll stay."

Chapter Two

Wyatt let out the breath he hadn't even realized he'd been holding. Relief rushed over him like a crisp, cool waterfall.

Carolina was going to stay.

Well—at least she was going to stay for a little while. And although her reasons might have nothing to do with him, he was determined to make it be about him and Matty. Which meant he had exactly two months to convince her she ought to make her permanent home in Haven, so he could be near his son for always. He knew it wouldn't be easy for him to see Carolina on a regular basis, but he would do anything for Matty.

That his initial encounter with Carolina hadn't gone over particularly well was hardly the point. What could she possibly have expected his reaction to be? Even after having an hour to get used to the idea of her arriving in town with their son—a boy he hadn't even known existed—in tow, he still felt like he'd been run over by a freight train, but with effort he'd taken that tornado of emotions and tucked it deep into his heart and out of sight. He was still angry and frustrated, and probably would be for a long time to come, but displaying how he felt wasn't going to help anyone, least of all Matty.

Wyatt had only been half listening to the conversation going on around him. His mind kept wandering to the dark-haired little boy who was probably even now exclaiming in delight over the horses.

Despite Wyatt's hurting heart, he couldn't help but smile at the thought of his son and being a daddy now. He could teach Matty how to ride a horse and buy him his own mount as soon as he learned to balance in the saddle. He would show his precious child everything about the world, introduce him to all the different kinds of farm and domestic animals he vetted and teach him all about life in the country.

One day, when he was all grown up, Matty even might want to become a veterinarian like his father. Wyatt would be proud to pass on his business to his son.

His *son.* That one word made his chest expand until he thought he might burst.

But he was getting a little ahead of himself.

Oh, who was he kidding? He was shooting off *way* ahead of himself.

First, he needed to get to know Matty, not to mention give the boy time to get comfortable with him. At some point—hopefully soon—he and Carolina would be able to explain to Matty that Wyatt was his daddy in a way a two-year-old could understand.

He was troubled by one thing. He had no idea how to go about being a good father. As a kid, he hadn't had a real male role model in his life. His parents had worked in a foreign aid office, and Wyatt had been raised solely by Gran.

He realized that while he had all of these idealistic notions about what a father should be, he didn't have a clue what was realistic and practical in everyday life.

It was unnerving to say the least, but no matter how much apprehension he felt inside, nothing would deter Wyatt from knowing his little boy and being part of Matty's life.

A big part.

He only hoped Carolina felt the same way. He was going to move forward with this either way, but it would certainly be easier if she wasn't fighting him at every turn. Did he dare assume that part of her reason for returning to Haven was that she had finally recognized that Wyatt had both the right and the responsibility to be in Matty's life? He knew she'd ostensibly come back to Haven to personally deliver the news of Morton Mason's death, but she could just as easily— actually, even more so—have sent an email to Bea. She hadn't had to come in person.

So maybe there *was* another reason she'd come back to town. Maybe it was for his sake—and Matty's.

Although that didn't explain why she had appeared so startled when she'd first seen him. Was that because he'd caught her off guard?

There were so many questions, and the only way to find the answers was to try to get along with Carolina—and cross his fingers that she would try to get along with him. At this point all he could do was hope for the best and step up for his role in this drama.

"I'm glad we got that all settled up," said the attorney, closing his briefcase with a snap that pulled Wyatt back to the present. "Thank you, Carolina, for agreeing to stay on here in Haven. I expect I speak for the Lone Star Cowboy League and the boys ranch when I say we appreciate your willingness to represent your family legacy at the seventieth-anniversary party. It may make all the difference to us and all the boys who call this place their home."

Carolina nodded. "Of course. I'm happy to do it."

Wyatt didn't think she sounded happy. He thought he still knew her well enough to distinguish the sadness in her voice. The grief.

And the stress.

Well, that made two of them.

Anyway, he really wasn't positive he knew Carolina all that well, if at all. Three years ago, he certainly hadn't anticipated that not only did she not reciprocate his feelings, but she'd run away from them, and while she was pregnant, no less.

No. He sighed inwardly. Three long years had passed between them. The truth was he probably didn't know the *real* Carolina Mason at all.

"We've still got one problem," Gabe said, cutting into Wyatt's thoughts about Carolina and their personal issues. "Even after searching extensively, I haven't been able to find my grandfather. At this point I'm not sure it's going to happen before the anniversary party."

Harold nodded gravely. "That is a problem."

Gabe planted his hat on his head and frowned. "I don't suppose you've got any enlightening letters for me in one of those file folders of yours."

"Actually, now that you mention it, there is a letter."

Gabe's eyes lit up with hope, but Harold's next words quickly doused that flame.

"It's not what you're hoping for. But it is based upon another contingency, and one that you all should know about. Especially you, Gabe. If, upon the morning of the seventieth-anniversary party, all of the men—and ladies," he said, tipping his Stetson to Carolina, "are not present and accounted for, I am to open the letter and read Cyrus's instructions on how to proceed with parceling out the land. I must caution you, it does not look promising. Obviously Cyrus had one thing and one thing only in mind when he wrote his will. So I encourage you to continue doing all you can to try to locate your grandfather before time runs out."

"Believe me, I am," Gabe said, his voice lowering in frustration. "So you're pretty much saying that the land will revert to the developer and half our boys will lose their places at the ranch."

Wyatt cringed in sympathy for his friend. Talk about a tough position to be in. He wouldn't want to be in Gabe's shoes right now, with the entire future of the boys ranch now dependent on his ability to find a man who had disappeared off the planet years ago.

Harold's steady gaze met Gabe's. "I'm not saying 'tis or 'tisn't. We won't know until I open the letter on the day of the party."

"At which point it will be too late for us to try to change things," Bea said with a groan, swiping a tired hand down her face.

"And that is exactly why we can't let that happen," Gabe said determinedly. "We've come too far to see this endeavor fall apart now. Somehow, I've got to find my grandfather and make this right."

"I know I'm new to all of this," Carolina said hesitantly, "but please feel free to call upon me if I can be of any assistance. I don't know what, if anything, I can do to help you, Gabe, but you've got my support any way you need it."

"Yeah," added Wyatt. "Same goes for me."

Wyatt's eyes met Carolina's and their eyes locked. They had their own set of problems to wade through, and the water was deep and murky.

Bea knocked her fist twice on the desk and stood, effectively ending the meeting. Folks started shuffling out of the office. Wyatt lingered so he could walk out directly after Carolina.

"I want to get to know my son," he said as soon as they cleared the building. "Spend some quality time with him."

The gaze Carolina flashed him was a combination of annoyance, frustration, hesitation and panic.

It was the hesitation that hit him hardest.

What? She didn't think he could handle Matty? That he didn't have it in him to be a father?

He frowned, all of his muscles tensing in response. He pressed his own fears aside in favor of feeling downright insulted by her attitude.

She didn't trust him with his own son? Granted, he knew nothing about children, but he'd been caring for animals all his life. He could be gentle.

If anything, *she* was the one who'd proven herself untrustworthy.

"Look. Not today," she said at last.

He clenched his fists to keep from barking out a rebuttal. At the moment, she was holding all the cards, and he felt entirely powerless.

"When, then?"

She sighed deeply, sounding bone weary. "I don't know, Wyatt. I just got into town. I haven't even set up house yet at my uncle's cabin, just a bunch of boxes in the living room and mattresses on the floor for Matty and me. It's going to take a while. And I'm still looking for a job."

"You're a registered nurse. You ought to be able to find employment around here easily enough. Have you checked at the hospital yet?"

Her eyes narrowed and she pursed her lips for a moment before answering. "Like I said—I'm looking. I'll let you know when I've found something suitable."

She sounded as if she doubted her own training and competence. Which was ridiculous. He might not be too thrilled with her personally right now, but he knew her to be an excellent nurse. She'd taken the very best care of his gran in her time of need, so much so that Gran had refused another nurse after Carolina had left.

Several other nurses, actually. No one could live up to the bar Carolina had set.

Surely any nearby medical facility would pick her up in a second. Nurses were always in shortage, especially good ones.

Maybe she was just trying to throw their conversation off track. He wasn't going to let that happen.

"Fine. I understand that you need to have the opportunity to work out all the details of your move to Haven. But I want an exact date and time when you will bring Matty to meet me, and it has to be soon."

"I said I don't know," she shot back, sounding thoroughly exasperated.

His dander rose. If she was irritated, that was all on her. He wasn't being unreasonable in asking for time to get to know his son.

Carolina blew out a breath. "I promise I'll call you just as soon as I get settled in. I suppose we can plan to set up a playdate at the park or something."

His eyebrows rose.

A *date*? Really?

If she thought he'd be going on *any* kind of date with her, she was sadly mistaken.

She looked at him questioningly and then burst into nervous laughter.

"I'm not asking you out, Wyatt. A playdate is when kids get together at the park. In this case, it will be you and your son. You can push him on the swing or play in the sandbox."

"Oh." He felt deflated, somehow. What was up with that? He knew he would have a great time with Matty, but—

"I have to go get Matty. I'm sure that Katie is rethinking her offer to watch him right about now. He can really be a handful when he gets excited, and I'm guessing he's over the moon about his first introduction to horses."

That should have been him. Yet another first that got away from him. Wyatt was determined it wouldn't happen again.

"But you'll call me, right?" Wyatt reiterated, knowing he was pushing her but beyond caring. "Soon?"

He wasn't sure *he* was ready to take on a handful of two-year-old energy any more than Katie was, but he would have to be ready. He would make himself ready.

He was a father now.

This was pointless.

Why was she even bothering to fill out an eight-page employment application at Haven's local nursing home and hospice? Carolina already knew she wasn't going to get the job. Probably not even an interview. She barely dared hope, and yet she had to try.

Thankfully, she didn't have to worry about Matty while she searched in vain for employment in the medical field. She and Katie were becoming good friends, and Katie had offered to watch Matty at the boys ranch office while Carolina went job hunting, as futile as it no doubt would be.

When had she become a cup-half-empty type of person?

Probably when her cup drained to its dregs and she hadn't seen a drop of liquid to fill it again.

No amount of previous background or additional skill sets could overcome the thorn in her side—or her knee, to be more accurate. She'd already been turned down by every other medical facility in the area, for the same reason she'd lost her job at the hospital in Colorado.

The need to be able to catch a fainting patient or respond to a slip and fall never even used to be a consideration for Carolina, much less a problem. She'd always kept herself in good shape with a gym membership that she actually used.

But then she'd made the mistake of going on a weekend ski trip with her roommate, Geena Walker. In hindsight, why she'd thought she ought to learn how to ski was beyond her comprehension. To be honest, she hadn't even really been all that interested in the sport. At the time it had seemed like a good idea, a fun way to take a short vacation and spend a weekend trying something new. She was living in Colorado, after all. Snow meant skiing, right?

She'd taken an hour's worth of quick instructional lessons, even though it was humiliating to be in a class of half-pint children who effortlessly picked up the necessary skills ten times faster than she did.

Afterward, she'd successfully skied the bunny slope a couple of times and *thought* she was ready to tackle a beginner's run.

It was easy, Geena had assured her. Simple as pie, she'd said. All Carolina had to do was ski from one side of the hill to the other in a diagonal fashion, slowly zigzagging her way down the mountainside.

Her first clue should have been when she slipped and nearly fell getting off the lift at the top of the mountain. But she'd chalked that up to being off balance and hit the slope.

Literally.

Neither Geena nor her ski instructor had mentioned what Carolina was supposed to do when her skis became crossed in the front and she went flipping head over heels for who knew how many yards down the snow-packed ski run.

All she remembered was not being able to breathe and feeling as if she were drowning in the snow, blinded by the icy white powder that had stolen inside her supposedly leak-proof goggles.

The next thing she knew, an entire crew of very young men sporting bright red jackets with white crosses embroidered on them surrounded her, insisting that they put her on a backboard and place a brace around her neck. She'd tried to tell them that she was a nurse and it wasn't necessary to overkill the situation, but they apparently wanted to practice their rescuing skills on her.

As if that wasn't bad enough, there was the humiliating turn down the hillside with all six of her escorts, while the regular skiers—the co-ordinated ones who didn't make themselves into human avalanches—watched on with interest.

As it happened, her back and neck were fine. Her left knee, however, not so much.

Then had come the surgery, rehabilitation and getting summarily dismissed from her job because of her inability to lift fifty pounds. And those doctor's orders weren't going anywhere any time soon.

Nope. They were permanent.

Which meant she was in permanent trouble.

Bringing her thoughts back to the present, she

sighed under her breath and scribbled her references on the employment application. Even if she already knew what the answer would be, she had to try.

Now that she had Wyatt breathing down her neck to spend time with Matty, it was more important than ever that she provide her son with a stable home, not only for his sake but to prove to Wyatt that she was able to make it on her own as a single mother.

That she didn't need his help.

Though she had started with every medical facility in the area, she didn't have time to be picky about where she worked. Even though she owned her great-uncle's cabin free and clear, she and Matty still needed to eat, and she had to pay to keep the lights on and put gas in the car.

Unfortunately for her, she wasn't really qualified for any other kind of work besides nursing. All of her education and expertise were the medical field. Retail or fast food might be an option in a pinch, but they didn't pay enough for her and Matty to subsist on in the long run. She needed a living wage, not a teenager's part-time after-school job. She supposed she could try to switch gears and become a medical receptionist, but her typing skills were atrocious and she'd never quite understood the medical filing system in the business classes she'd had to take in college.

Carolina closed her eyes and said a silent prayer. She'd been praying a lot more often recently, asking the Lord for guidance, not only in her career, but in her life. And now, more than anything, she needed direction on what she should do about her relationship—or lack of one—with Wyatt Harrow.

She was just about out of options.

Please, dear Lord, don't make me have to beg.

Carolina was handing in her application at the front desk when, to her surprise, she spotted Wyatt out of the corner of her eye. She would have recognized his long, confident gait anywhere, not to mention his handsome profile.

Though he'd come in through the main glass doors of the nursing home, he clearly hadn't seen her. He was walking down a hallway with his head down and his hands crammed into the front pockets of his jeans.

Even at a distance, and even though she couldn't see the expression on his face, Carolina could tell he was troubled from his posture alone. She'd seen that look before, when his gran had been having so much trouble.

It was none of her business. She should leave now, before he turned around and recognized her. That would be the sensible thing to do. The smart thing.

But her days of doing the sensible thing were long behind her.

Instead, curiosity got the better of her and she followed him down the hallway, taking care to stay a few steps behind him and ready to duck into a doorway if he looked back.

Happily, he didn't. He took a right, then an immediate left, and then he disappeared into a room on the right side of the hallway.

Carolina paused. What Wyatt was doing had nothing to do with her, but—

She had to look.

She just had to.

She continued down the hall straight past where Wyatt had gone, quickening her pace as she glanced into the room. She felt silly, like a teenage girl stalking her first crush around the halls in high school.

When she saw Wyatt sitting in a chair next to an old woman's bedside, her heart swelled and then melted like warm chocolate.

Of course.

Wyatt was visiting his gran. No wonder he'd looked so burdened. Eva Harrow had clearly gone downhill from when Carolina had last seen her.

Carolina was more than a little bit familiar with Wyatt's grandmother, having been the old woman's home nurse for several months three years ago, just before Carolina had left Haven.

That was how she'd gotten to know Wyatt and when she had fallen in love with him. He clearly cared so much for his grandmother—such an attractive trait in a man.

Eva had accidentally plunged down a set of porch steps and had broken her hip. At that time in her life, it had become clear that her dementia was slowly overtaking her. Wyatt had needed Carolina's round-the-clock help to keep Eva safe, but at that time he wouldn't even consider putting her in a nursing home where she could get the kind of medical assistance she needed on a more permanent basis.

Eva was also—indirectly—the reason Matty had been conceived. One evening a few months into Carolina's work for the Harrows, Wyatt's gran had taken a sudden turn for the worse and spiked a high fever. She had ended up in the ICU with pneumonia and little chance of recovering. In his grief, Wyatt had turned to Carolina for comfort.

Carolina breathed deeply as memories flooded over her. Eva had managed to fight off a bad infection, although it was touch and go there for a while. She was one of the strongest people Carolina had ever had the privilege of knowing, but the woman had been ninety-six at the time of her injury and there was only so much recovery she could make, especially considering how quickly her dementia was changing her world for the worse.

But Wyatt hadn't been ready to let her go then—or even now, apparently. Her heart welled as she watched him interact with her. He was holding Eva's hand and speaking in a loud, animated tone of voice. Carolina was fairly certain from Eva's blank-eyed, slack-featured expression that she did not recognize Wyatt at all.

Still, she appeared to be listening to him intently and wasn't pulling away from his touch, so it was at least the semblance of a good day for her.

"Did I tell you about the donkey Johnny and I rescued? You remember I told you about Johnny, right? He's the teenager I'm mentoring. Anyway, the whole thing with the donkey was so funny. We pulled him out of the mud bog he was stuck in, and I kid you not, Gran, that animal grinned from ear to ear when we freed him. A donkey smiling. Can you imagine? And you should have heard him braying a thank-you."

Wyatt laughed at his own story, then paused, his expression drawing serious.

"Johnny really means a lot to me. I feel like I can help him, you know?" He scoffed and shook his head. "Life doesn't always work out the way we plan, huh, Gran? I thought by now I would be overseas somewhere, helping people out there, but instead I—well, there's Johnny. And you, of course. I'd never leave you. And—" Wyatt's voice caught in his throat and he paused.

And then he glanced up.

His gaze locked with Carolina's, and her adrenaline spiked, rushing through her.

She'd been made.

It was her own fault, of course, for standing in the middle of the doorway gawking at him, eavesdropping on his time with his gran. But that didn't stop embarrassment from flooding her cheeks.

"Carolina."

"Eh?" Eva said, clearly confused as she turned her head to look at Carolina.

"I—er—was just passing by and I thought I heard your voice." Carolina cringed inwardly. Now there was a lame excuse if she'd ever heard one.

"You were just strolling through the nursing home for no reason?"

"Well, no. Not exactly."

"What, then? *Exactly?*" He paused and narrowed his gaze on her, appraising her. "You weren't following me around, now, were you?"

She froze and she was sure she was gaping.

He laughed.

She let out a breath, glad he'd only been kidding about the idea of her following him around.

Even if, technically, she kind of was.

She didn't want to have to explain to him that she was still looking for work. It was so incredibly important that he perceive her as having a stable, successful life, even if in reality her existence was anything but. She didn't want to give herself away.

"Mind your manners, young man," Eva scolded. She shook a finger at Wyatt and then turned her gaze on Carolina. "Did you bring me any water?"

"I'd be happy to get you a glass of water." Her emotions overflowed with love for Eva. It broke her heart that she'd ever had to leave the woman in the first place. But what choice had she had?

And worse, she'd assumed that Eva would have passed on by now. She hadn't even asked Wyatt about her. Guilt singed her at the thought.

Wyatt caught her eyes and briefly shook his head.

"I have a case of bottled water in the trunk," he explained. "I always fill up her mini fridge when I visit. I have to unscrew all the lids so she can open them herself whenever she gets thirsty."

"I'm thirsty," Eva repeated, although she didn't appear to be following Wyatt and Carolina's conversation.

"See if there's a bottle left in the fridge," Wyatt suggested. "Gran, I've brought you your favorite kind of chocolate. Dark chocolate truffles. Do you want to see?"

While Wyatt helped his grandmother unwrap a piece of candy, Carolina went to the fridge for a bottle of water. She took off the lid and handled the bottle to Eva.

"How long has she been living here?"

Wyatt's brow lowered. "Since just after you disappeared. I couldn't find a home-care nurse she liked after you left. She compared every one of them to you, and then she would scare 'em all off within the first week or so."

He wasn't pointing a finger of blame at her, although he had every right to do just that, but he appeared troubled by the memory, and Carolina was sorry she'd brought it up.

"Her one hundredth birthday is near the end of this month," he said, still looking disturbed but trying to move on. "I've been thinking about throwing her a big birthday bash so all her friends and neighbors can wish her a happy one, but I'm not sure I should. I can never anticipate if she's going to have a good day. She probably wouldn't recognize any of the guests, and it might agitate her instead of making her happy."

"Oh, you should do it," Carolina enthused, unable to help herself. "Living to be one hundred years old is an enormous accomplishment and it should be celebrated, not only by her, but by her friends. Even if she doesn't recognize any-one, I'm sure she'll enjoy knowing so many people care about her. I'll help you plan the party if you'd like."

His jaw tightened and he shook his head. "How would you know what Gran would like?" he snapped and then quickly lowered his voice when Eva frowned at him. "You left us—*her*—high and dry."

He might as well have slapped her face. His words had the same impact.

"No. You're right. I'm sorry. I'm sticking my nose where it doesn't belong. Forget I said anything."

For all she knew, he might be able to forget about what she'd said, and maybe even forget about her, Carolina thought, her gut tightening in misery.

But she wouldn't. Three years ago, when she'd left Haven, she'd walked away from her heart, her home and her life.

Now she had returned, only to find her life immeasurably more complicated.

Was there anything left for her here?

seem fair that his intelligent, lively gran could be reduced to this shell of a woman.

He visited her once a week, on Monday mornings. At first, after he'd made the painful decision to place Gran in the nursing home, he'd tried to visit every other day or so. But more often than not, his appearance upset her or sent her into a flurry of mindless activity, so he'd eventually lessened his visits. It hurt his heart, but this wasn't about him.

Most of the time when he visited, Gran didn't recognize him at all. Sometimes she thought he was Grandpa George, or Wyatt's father, Ian. Occasionally, she was completely lucid and knew exactly who he was. Sometimes, like today, she had no idea what his name was but sensed he was connected to her in some way.

And then there were the times he hated the most, when his presence disturbed her, or she would beg for him to take her home with him. He didn't know whether or not to be thankful that she recognized him less and less frequently. He didn't like to see her unhappy.

Always, it was an emotional roller coaster for Wyatt. He knew he had been blessed to have his grandmother with him as long as he had, but the thought of the world without her in it still saddened and pained him.

"Does she like any specific soap operas or

Chapter Three

Wyatt wasn't convinced he should have welcomed Carolina into the room. Maybe he should have tossed her out on her ear. He wasn't even quite clear on why she was there in the first place. He couldn't believe she would take to following him around. More likely that she was here applying for a job.

He watched her speaking to Gran, rearranging the old woman's pillows and locating the television remote for her. Carolina was good at her job. No—she was excellent. Gran was relaxed and responsive, better than she usually was around Wyatt or any of the other nurses at the facility.

Wyatt hated the disease that had eroded his precious gran's mind, leaving her perpetually confused about not only where she was, but who she was. That was the nature of the beast. It didn't game shows?" Carolina asked, pointing the remote toward the television and clicking through the channels at random.

"She likes those court shows," he replied. "You know, the ones with the judges pounding their gavels, where people fight over stupid stuff?"

"Right." Carolina turned to a channel where a black-robed judge was sitting behind a bench barking out a sentence to a miserable plaintiff and an elated defendant.

"There you go, Eva," Carolina said, her voice soft and affectionate. "How's that for you? The judges are funny, aren't they?"

Gran reached out and patted Carolina's cheek. "You are such a sweetheart."

Wyatt's stomach tightened. He used to believe that, too. It galled him to think he could be so wrong about a person, especially as close as he'd thought he'd been to Carolina.

He must be the worst judge of character ever. He should just stick to the animals. At least with them a man always knew where he stood.

Animals were loyal.

But Carolina?

She'd certainly put on a good show for him three years ago, when they'd been dating and when he'd believed he was in love with her. She was a consummate actress—he could say that about her. He'd bought her performance hook, line and sinker, believing that she was the sweetest, kindest, most beautiful woman in the world.

Believing she was the only woman in the world for him. That they were meant to be together. That he wanted to put a ring on her finger and make his love for her permanent.

That their love would last forever.

What love?

Had she ever loved him, or had it all been his imagination and a desperate need for her to feel as he did?

He still thought she was beautiful, at least on the outside. That hadn't changed. How could it?

But as for the rest of it? That woman had never existed at all, or else she wouldn't have disappeared without one word to him when she got pregnant with his child.

What kind of a person even did that?

Not the same woman who was carrying on a quiet conversation with his gran. It was hard to reconcile what he was seeing before him.

Watching Carolina now, it was as if the years had fallen away. Sweet, sensitive Carolina had always been able to calm Gran, had always appeared to know exactly what the old woman required even when Gran couldn't voice her needs. Carolina knew how to react to any given situation without losing her composure.

Those qualities were what had made her such

a good nurse, and those qualities were among those that had initially caught his eye, and eventually his heart.

He and Carolina had laughed together, cried together, and in a moment of deepest grief, they had ultimately found temporary solace in each other's arms. And while Wyatt hadn't intended for things to happen in that order, their night together had only strengthened his resolve, solidified the love between them—or at least that's what he'd thought at the time.

He had already had the ring and had been ready to propose to her. Even before that night, he'd known he wanted to spend his life with her.

He could have made it right—for all three of them—if only she would have let him. If only she would have stayed. If only she had been honest with him from the beginning.

Wyatt scoffed softly and stood abruptly, striding to the window overlooking a tree-lined greenbelt. It didn't make any sense. Not one bit of it. There wasn't anything rational about the things Carolina had done and had failed to do, before or since she had left him three years ago.

There was no way to reconcile the woman he'd thought he'd loved, the one who even now obviously cared deeply for his gran, with the woman who had callously left him in the lurch without a thought to how he would feel. Without considering that he had rights and responsibilities as a dad.

Or that Matty needed a father.

"Why are you here?" he asked without turning. He wasn't entirely certain what he was asking. Why was she here today, in Gran's room, for starters? But in truth it was so much more than one thing. Nothing was that simple anymore.

Was this visit about Gran? Had Carolina somehow discovered this was where Wyatt had placed Gran when he could no longer take care of her? Was she here to visit her? Was it purely an accident that she'd encountered Wyatt?

But no. She'd looked totally stricken—*guilty*— when he'd first spotted her in the doorway, silently observing him with Gran. Her face had turned twenty shades of red at least. She'd looked just as shocked when her gaze shifted to his grandmother as it had when their eyes had met.

But if this wasn't about Gran, then what was it, really?

"I was filling out an employment application," she replied reluctantly.

"Oh?" He swiveled on his heel, leaned his hip on the windowsill and crossed his arms. "I figured you'd probably go for a job at the hospital. I'm sure it pays better."

Color rose in her face once again, flaming her cheeks. What was she not telling him? Her unspoken words hung in the air between them until she dropped her gaze.

"I don't know why I bothered coming out here today. They won't hire me, any more than the hospital."

"What? Why not?" Whatever else Carolina was or wasn't, she was a competent, compassionate nurse. She'd been in the top of her class in college and had an outstanding résumé.

"I don't meet the physical qualifications."

Now that he *really* didn't believe. Carolina was petite, but she was in perfect physical condition. She had a runner's slim stature and she'd been a regular at the gym in all the time that he'd known her. A man couldn't be breathing and not notice her shapely form.

"I trashed my knee in a skiing accident a few months back. I had to have surgery on it, and it's still liable to give way on me at any moment. I can't trust it, and neither can a prospective employer. Doctor's orders that I don't lift too much weight. I can't blame the facilities for turning me away."

"I'm sorry to hear that," he said, and meant it. "Are you in any pain?"

She smiled, but it was sad and forlorn, matching the anguish in her eyes. "Sometimes. But more than the physical pain is not being able to do what I love to do. Nursing, not skiing," she qualified.

He chuckled, but his mind was spinning, trying to process this new information. If she couldn't find a job, then she couldn't support Matty. She wouldn't even be able to support *herself*.

Wyatt might not like what she had done to him, but she was still the mother of his child, and there was no question that he would take care of her and Matty, as much as they needed for as long as they needed.

"How can I help?"

She squared her shoulders and raised her chin. "I don't need any assistance from you."

He scrubbed a hand through his hair. There was pride, and then there was sheer stubbornness.

"Look, if you need some money or something to help you get by…"

"No." Carolina spoke so forcefully that Gran looked away from her show to eye both of them dubiously.

Carolina lowered her voice. "Thank you for offering, but I don't need your help," she repeated. "I've been taking care of Matty since he was born, and I'll do it now. I'll find a job. You don't have to worry about us. Matty and I will be just fine."

She was face-to-face with him now, close enough that he could feel her breath fanning his cheek.

He wanted to be angry at her words, at the

callous way she'd dismissed him from her and Matty's lives. But despite his best efforts, his rebellious senses bolted to life, as if they'd been lying dormant for years. Every awareness amplified, from the breezy, floral scent of her perfume to the way he knew she would fit perfectly under the crook of his shoulder if he were to move forward just the tiniest bit.

He took a big step backward.

Was he *insane*?

This was the woman who had run off with his son. What he should be thinking about, what was imperative, was that Matty—and by extension, Carolina—had what they needed, not only to survive, but to thrive.

The problem was convincing Carolina he wasn't offering charity. It was his responsibility to look after them, but he was fairly certain she wouldn't see it that way.

"Promise me you won't wait too long before asking." His voice was unusually husky. "And that if you or Matty are ever in need—of anything, Carolina, and I mean that—you'll come to me first."

Her eyes widened and she pinched her lips into a tight line. She shook her head and reached for her purse, which she'd set on Gran's nightstand when she entered.

"I assure you that won't be necessary." She

flashed a tense smile for Gran's sake and gave her a quick peck on the cheek. "I'll be back to visit you soon, Eva."

The next moment she was gone, without so much as another word to Wyatt.

How fittingly reminiscent of her.

"Thank you anyway, Dr. Delgado. I appreciate you calling me back." Carolina ended the call, sighed deeply and clasped her cell phone—one item she wouldn't be able to afford after the end of this month—tightly to her chest.

She squeezed her eyes closed, but tears surfaced despite her best efforts, making slow, silent streams down her cheeks. She slipped her cell phone into the back pocket of her jeans and groaned in frustration.

Thankfully Matty was absorbed in the preschool programming he was watching on television, counting along with the colorful aliens who were surreptitiously teaching him math skills in the form of entertainment.

Carolina sniffed and wiped her wet cheeks with her palm.

That was it, then. Her last hope for local employment in the medical field. Dr. Delgado had let her down kindly, but he already had two long-term employees, a registered nurse and a physician's assistant. Doc had wished Carolina well but had offered no further suggestions on where she might look for a job.

She was out of options. She was out of money. And she was out of time.

She was grateful she owned Uncle Mort's cabin free and clear, but he hadn't had much else in the way of assets, and now was dipping into her meager savings account every time she visited the grocery store or wrote a check for utilities. Her unemployment benefits didn't begin to cover their necessities. Matty had hit another growth spurt, and all of his jeans were inches too short at the ankles. She had been looking around for viable day care options for him, but she didn't want to skimp on that expense. Matty deserved the very best care available. And next year he'd be in preschool, with a whole new set of challenges.

Not that she had a need for day care until she managed to find employment. She scoffed aloud.

Lord, what would You have me do?

She had no choice but to stay in Haven, at least for the next couple of months, and it wasn't as if she really had any better options elsewhere. She was as stuck in the mud as that donkey Wyatt had been telling his gran about.

After checking on Matty, Carolina tucked one leg under her on a kitchen chair and opened her laptop, a spiral notebook and a ballpoint pen beside her to make a record of her online applications. She was determined to check every local internet job board for postings.

At this point she was willing to consider anything. She didn't care how overqualified she might be. Beggars couldn't afford to be choosers, especially when that particular beggar had a growing boy to care for.

A half hour later, having found not a single lead or typed in a single application, she put Matty down for his afternoon nap, lingering to gaze at his sweet face, so pure and innocent in sleep.

Matty didn't deserve any of this. She had already made so many wrong choices during his young life. Carolina wanted to offer her son the world, but at this point she could barely offer him his next meal.

Promise you won't wait too long before asking.

Wyatt's words echoed through her mind, taunting her.

If Matty is ever in need, come to me first.

No.

How could she even be considering taking Wyatt up on his offer?

But then again, how could she not?

If she only had to worry about herself, she'd starve before she asked for a handout. But it wasn't her she was thinking about.

It was Matty.

Even if she went door to door among Haven businesses trying to find a job—as it appeared she would have to do, since she had found no leads online—it would take her time to connect with something, and another couple of weeks after that to get her first paycheck.

She was desperate enough to consider anything, up to and including flipping hamburgers or waitressing at the local truck stop. But she wasn't entirely convinced even the fast-food joints around town would be interested in hiring her.

Wyatt had a steady, good-paying job in Haven, and had since the day he'd graduated from veterinary school. He hadn't said anything about a wife, and he wasn't wearing a wedding ring, so presumably he didn't have a family to care for, other than his gran. He probably had plenty of extra savings to fall back on.

More than she did, anyway.

He was Matty's father.

And he had offered.

But could she do it?

The moment she'd arrived back in Haven and had come face-to-face with Wyatt, she'd been in a perpetual cycle of eating humble pie.

Choking on it, more like.

What was one more interaction in the big scheme of things? If Wyatt truly wanted to be a part of Matty's life, then providing for some of his physical needs was as good a start as any.

With a sigh, Carolina leaned over the toddler bed to brush a kiss over the soft skin of Matty's forehead.

She couldn't even believe she was seriously considering asking Wyatt for help. She was *not* a charity case—and if she was going to do this, she would make absolutely certain that Wyatt understood she wasn't asking for her own good. Nor would she take a single thing for herself.

This was all about Matty.

She slumped back into the chair at the kitchen table and wiggled her mouse to open the screen again, hoping beyond hope that in the five minutes it had taken to put Matty down for his nap, the perfect job might have somehow suddenly popped onto the top of the employment board.

It hadn't.

Which meant she had no choice but to call Wyatt.

She fished her cell phone out of the back pocket of her jeans, unlocked the screen and paused, staring at the background picture for a long moment.

It was a photo she'd taken of Matty when her previous roommate Geena's then boyfriend and now husband had given Matty his Colorado Rockies baseball hat. Matty had been grinning from ear to ear as the bill of the oversize black-and-purple cap dipped low over one eye.

After the first picture, Geena had then turned the hat backward. At that moment, Carolina remembered being struck by how much Matty looked like his father. Wyatt often wore a backward-facing baseball cap when he was out tending to the animals he vetted.

Her stomach knotted as she thumbed through her contact list to where Wyatt's cell phone number was located. Wyatt was no longer first on her quick-dial list, but though she'd considered doing it many times, she'd never quite been able to bring herself to delete his number entirely.

She was a sentimental fool.

She sniffed softly and shook her head. There was no sense putting off the inevitable.

Wyatt's phone rang four times before he picked up. Carolina was just about to end the call when she heard his voice. She figured he'd probably seen her name on his caller ID and decided he didn't want to speak with her just then. Or maybe at all. And this wasn't the sort of conversation she could leave as a message.

"Carolina?"

Hearing her name on Wyatt's lips jarred her. She gulped in surprise and nearly punched the end button.

"Yes. It's m-me." She stammered to a halt, trying to gather her thoughts.

"How are you settling in?" he asked when she didn't immediately continue.

It was a leading question in any number of ways.

She let out her breath. "Um—that's why I'm calling, actually."

There. She'd said it.

"Great. So when can I see Matty?"

It took her a moment to realize he was referring to her promise to call him once she was settled in, in order to set up a playdate.

She was *so* not ready.

"Actually, I was wondering if I could talk to you about something."

A lengthy pause followed and Carolina's throat hitched.

"Sure. Okay. What's up?"

It hurt to release the air from her lungs, like breathing frost on a cold day. "It's not really something I want to discuss over the phone. Would it be okay if I meet you at your office?"

"Well, all right. I guess so. I'm out on a house call right now, but I should be back in the office in an hour. Will that be okay for you?"

"Yes, that will actually work out great. That will give me some time to find someone to watch Matty for me while I'm visiting with you."

"You're not bringing him with you?" His clipped voice lowered.

"Not this time. Please, Wyatt. I need to speak to you alone. I promise we'll set something up with Matty, but not right now."

"In an hour, then." Wyatt ended the call without so much as a goodbye.

Carolina stared at her cell phone's orange screen flashing Call Ended and sighed.

This wasn't going to go well. He was already upset with her, and what she was about to tell him was only going to make things worse.

If only she had any other options...

But she didn't.

She phoned Katie, who cheerfully agreed to drop by and watch Matty while Carolina conducted what she had nicknamed her *unfortunate business*. It was better than, say, *begging*. She was appreciative of her friend, who was always ready to pitch in without asking too many questions. When she got back on her feet, she'd have to buy Katie a nice bouquet of flowers or something as a thank-you gift.

Forty-five minutes later, Carolina was waiting outside Wyatt's office, rubbing her suddenly clammy palms against the denim of her blue jeans.

Wyatt opened the door before she could knock, his expression a composite of sharp planes and hard lines. He stepped out of the doorway and gestured her inside.

"Sorry about the mess," he apologized as he followed her through the door. "My administrative assistant moved away about six months ago and somehow I haven't gotten around to hiring a new one. I thought I might have—" he paused "—moved on by now. Started an office elsewhere."

So he was still planning to leave town. Carolina had interpreted his conversation with his gran to mean he still had plans abroad, but here was definite confirmation.

Which only served to complicate matters even worse. She had no idea what to do with Wyatt's relationship with Matty. She only knew she didn't want her son to be hurt, as she had been by her own father, a man who was out of her life more than he was in. He'd pop in for a weekend or two, take her out someplace fun so she'd think well of him, and then disappear for months. She often thought it would have been better for her had he simply not been there at all.

"Please, sit," he said, plucking a pile of file folders off a metal folding chair.

Wyatt's office was no more than an offshoot of the barn on his home property, where he kept not only his own animals, but any under his care who needed close observation. The L-shaped cherrywood desk fit into the back corner, flanked on one side by a metal filing cabinet and on the other by a printer.

Stacks of papers and invoices covered every flat surface in the room. It looked like he hadn't filed since his administrative assistant had left.

He lifted his Stetson and slicked a hand back through his black hair.

"I had no idea I would have to deal with so much paperwork when I became a vet. It looks like I should have minored in accounting. I keep meaning to get through this mess, but every time I try, I get called away on an emergency. Or I decide I'd rather take the day off and stream a show on television," he joked.

Her forced chuckle sounded like a witch's cackle and she cut it off short.

He took a seat on a swivel chair that looked as if it had seen better days.

"So what's up?" He leaned forward and rested his forearms on his knees, clasping his hands in front of him. "Is Matty faring all right with the move? I know it can be a little disconcerting to find yourself in new surroundings with a bunch of strangers."

"Yes, he's—" Carolina began, but then she shook her head and blew out a breath. "No. He's not fine."

Wyatt jerked to his feet, concern clouding his features. He looked ready to do—something.

What? Climb aboard his trusty white steed and ride in to save the day?

Unfortunately, that was exactly what she was about to ask him to do.

"Wait. There's no cause for worry." She held up her hands and waved him back to his seat. "I'm sorry. This isn't coming out right. There's nothing wrong with Matty. That is—"

Her sentence drifted off into silence. This was *way* harder than she'd anticipated, and she'd already been certain it was going to be excruciatingly painful.

"I haven't been able to find a job," she forced out. "And it's not for want of looking."

She dropped her gaze. She just couldn't stand to look into Wyatt's eyes and admit she was a failure as a mom. To see the *I told you so* in his stare.

"I see." He leaned back and crossed his arms.

"Employment as a nurse, I mean. I'm still actively looking for something—anything, at this point, really—and I'm sure it won't be long before a job of some sort comes up, but in the meantime—"

"You'd like me to help you support Matty."

Wyatt could certainly be blunt when he wanted to be. She felt like he'd just stabbed her in the heart.

Repeatedly.

"Carolina." His voice was surprisingly tender. She didn't know what she had expected.

Anger. Frustration. Disgust, even.

Just not this.

She couldn't handle the gentleness that made him so good as a vet. It was the one emotion she had no armor strong enough to resist.

He tipped up her chin with his index finger.

"I will give Matty—and you—whatever you need."

"Don't worry about me," she said, her stubborn streak rising despite knowing that this whole meeting depended on her remaining humble and taking whatever Wyatt dished out.

"No, Carolina. That's not how this goes. I'm going to help both of you, any way I can. I have total confidence that you'll find a decent job and get back on your feet in no time."

"You do?" she asked through a dry throat.

"I do. But whether or not you're employed, I am Matty's father. I have both a right and a responsibility to contribute to his support, financially and in every other way."

"I never meant for you—"

"To find out I had a son?" he cut in brusquely.

"That's not what I was going to say."

"Good. Then it's settled."

He crouched down before the bottom drawer of the file cabinet and opened it. She couldn't see what he was doing, but there were several metallic clicks and bumps.

After a moment, he stood up and turned around, his hand now full of hundred-dollar bills. Carolina guessed he held close to two thousand dollars.

Her eyes widened, and she was fairly certain she was gaping. When she had asked for help, she hadn't meant two months of total support. A small loan was all.

"Wyatt, I can't take this."

"Of course you can. It's only a couple thousand dollars. I'm sure I'm further behind on my child support payments than that."

"No. You've got this all wrong. I don't expect you to try to make up for—"

He held up a hand and laughed drily.

"That was a joke. Not a very good one, apparently."

He reached for her hand and tucked the bills into her palm, closing her fingers around the money. When he pulled back, his elbow hit a stack of invoices, sending papers floating to the floor in every direction.

Wyatt groaned. "Oh, great. And wouldn't you know those were the ones I already had in a semblance of order."

Despite herself, Carolina chuckled.

"I think maybe you need a little help."

"More than a little," he agreed, and then his eyes lit up and he cocked his head at her.

He paused for so long that she shifted uncomfortably under his gaze.

"Can you file?"

"Can't everyone?" She raised her eyebrows. "Unless you're talking about medical filing, which is a whole other thing. But regular filing? That's just a matter of knowing your ABCs, right? And I've been consistently practicing them with Matty since the time he was six months old. I'm officially a pro."

"You're hired."

"I'm—" she sputtered. "Excuse me, what?"

"You're hired," he repeated, his grin widening. "It's the perfect solution."

"What's perfect?" She wasn't following his train of thought at *all*, and from the gratified expression on Wyatt's face, she wasn't certain she wanted to know *what* he was thinking.

"The answer to both of our dilemmas. I need help organizing my pathetic excuse for an office, and you need a job. I'll pay you the going rate for an administrative assistant and you won't be accepting charity."

"Yes, but—"

She'd been going to protest that she was thoroughly unqualified for the position, but hadn't she just this morning decided she would take whatever she could get? And really, how hard could it be?

In truth, working as his administrative assistant wasn't a half-bad idea. If it were anyone except Wyatt, she knew she would be jumping all over this opportunity.

But it *was* Wyatt who was offering.

Could she really work alongside him as if they had no past together? As if they didn't share a son?

Could she manage the emotions she knew would sneak up on her when she wasn't paying attention?

"I'll sweeten the pot." He looked enthusiastic, maybe even a little smug.

Her eyes narrowed on him. He was making this way too easy for her.

"How?"

"Have you made arrangements for Matty's day care yet?" He crossed his arms and leaned his hip against the desk, looking casually at ease.

Which was the exact opposite of how she was feeling right now. Her shoulders tightened as he pointed out yet another of her recent failings.

"I'm working on it," she admitted cautiously.

Could his grin *get* any wider?

Her frown deepened, directly mirroring the spreading of his smile.

"You can bring Matty with you to the office.

You won't have child care expenses, and I'll be able to spend some time getting to know my son better. What do you say, Carolina?"

He rocked forward in anticipation of her answer. He looked as hopeful as a boy on his first fishing trip, holding his pole and waiting for a bite.

What could she say?

Wyatt deserved to know his son. She knew that. But how could she protect Matty's heart if Wyatt was ultimately going to leave him behind?

On the other hand, she needed the job and someone to watch Matty. In his determination to get to know his son, Wyatt had offered her the answer to both dilemmas. At least this way she would be in the room to supervise their interactions.

But even knowing it was the right thing to do, she still had to force the words through tight lips.

"I think we'd better set up that playdate."

Chapter Four

Wyatt had never been so nervous in his life. He'd arrived at the park fifteen minutes early so he could observe other parents on the playground interacting with their children.

Being slung so unexpectedly into fatherhood would be enough to rattle any man, but Wyatt was an only child who had been raised by his grandmother. As a boy he'd hung out with animals more than people. What he didn't know about toddlers could fill an encyclopedia set.

The only kids he'd ever spent any time with were of the baby goat variety. What if he messed up with Matty? What if he didn't have what it took to be a dad?

He watched a young father spotting his little girl down a slide. The child was giggling and her dad looked completely relaxed and carefree.

Wyatt was neither. He felt sick to his stomach and like he was about to jump out of his skin.

Ready, set, go.

Whether he was ready or not.

Carolina waved as she approached, holding a squirming Matty with her other hand. Matty had seen the playground and was clearly eager to unload some energy on it. The moment she let the boy loose, he barreled toward a spring-loaded rocket, climbed aboard and pumped back and forth with as much force as his little arms and legs could manage.

Carolina still appeared reticent about this meeting, but he supposed he should have expected that. He had no regrets about hiring her for his office, although maybe she did, after she'd returned home and had had time to think about it.

In his mind, anything that meant he would have more time with his son was a good thing, even if he was still struggling to completely wrap his mind around the idea of Carolina now also being a permanent part of his life—at least, he hoped that would be true. He still worried that she had no intention of staying in Haven permanently, that he would get to know Matty just in time for her to take him away again.

For the first few minutes, Carolina said nothing to him at all, just folded her arms as if she were chilled and silently watched Matty as he moved from the rocket to a small tower. Made for the younger children, there were no holes or gaps for them to fall into. It had steps rather than climbing bars and a small straight slide, compared to the long spiral slide the larger tower held.

For the moment, Matty appeared safe enough on his own. Wyatt thought maybe he ought to be doing something, interacting with Matty in some way like he'd seen the father of the little girl doing, but he had no idea what to do, and Carolina wasn't giving him any guidance.

After what seemed like forever, Matty dashed back in their direction.

"Swing, Mama."

Carolina glanced at Wyatt and her mouth curved into a grin. "You want to take this?"

Wyatt tried to swallow but his throat was too dry.

"S-sure," he stammered.

"Come on, Matty. Mr. Wyatt is going to push you on the swing, okay?"

Matty didn't appear to care who pushed him, as long as he got to swing.

"Use one of the toddler swings—the ones that support him around the middle."

He was grateful Carolina was finally offering him a little instruction instead of leaving him to stumble his way through his first interaction with his son. Maybe this wouldn't be so difficult, after all.

"May I pick you up, little man?" he asked Matty, holding out his hands to the boy.

He half expected Matty to run in the other direction, cower behind Carolina's legs or jump into her arms and hide his head in her shoulder as he had the first time they'd met, but this time Matty didn't hesitate. He climbed right into Wyatt's arms without a protest.

Wyatt couldn't help but smile as he threaded Matty's plump legs into the seat of the swing.

He was playing with his son!

The emotions stirring in his chest were beyond imagining. Love and pride dueled for precedence at the front of the pack, but there were so many other things, too. Was this how it would always feel when he looked at Matty?

He gave the swing a little push, then another, careful not to go beyond a couple of feet in either direction.

"Higher! Higher!" Matty called impatiently, pumping his legs and rocking back and forth in the swing.

Wyatt's gaze shifted to Carolina.

She chuckled and nodded.

He pushed a little harder, but Matty continued to beg for more.

"You're going to have to do better than that,"

Carolina said. "He's a real daredevil. He likes to go as high as the swing will carry him."

"Isn't that dangerous?"

Her eyes widened, as if she'd never even considered the possibility. Maybe she hadn't, and he was being foolish. He didn't have the built-in daddy sensor that he assumed other men had.

"I don't think so," she responded slowly. "The chair keeps him from tipping over, and as you can see, he has a good grip on the chains. So unless you're intending to swing him in a three-hundred-sixty-degree circle, I don't think we have to worry about him falling out."

Heat traveled up Wyatt's neck and into his face. He was an idiot. Why hadn't he noticed the way the parents around him were acting? One young woman was only half paying attention as she pushed her child on a nearby swing while simultaneously texting on her cell phone.

No one looked alarmed or nervous.

Was he going to overreact to every situation in which he found himself with Matty? He didn't want to be that hovering, overprotective father, but he couldn't help the way his heart jerked into his throat when he pulled Matty out of the swing chair and the boy immediately headed toward a geometric dome made up of metal pipes. The pipes had to be slippery and the holes between the triangles were easily large enough for his two-year-old son to fall through.

"He's fine," Carolina assured Wyatt with a smile, even though he hadn't shared any of his thoughts and fears aloud. "He climbs like a monkey. Swings like one, too. And he likes bananas," she teased.

Be that as it may, Wyatt inched closer to what appeared to him to be an entirely unsafe piece of playground equipment. He wasn't about to let Matty fall.

Dads were supposed to be the ones to encourage their sons to reach higher, try harder, be strong and courageous. He was hovering over Matty like a mother hen.

Maybe—hopefully Wyatt would get to the point where he could trust himself to do the right thing, where he instinctively knew how to be a daddy. But right now he felt like he was walking over hot coals with bare feet.

"You should have seen me the first time I brought Matty to the playground." Carolina laughed and laid a hand on Wyatt's shoulder. "I was spotting him so closely that there was no way he could have fallen off anything. I was positive the other parents were laughing at me as I followed him around with inches to spare."

Wyatt shoved his hands into his pockets. Was it

that easy for Carolina to read what he was thinking just from his expression alone?

Back when they were dating, she used to have an uncanny knack for guessing the emotions he was experiencing and knowing just what to say or do to make him feel better. She'd had the same gift with Gran.

Except for the part when he'd realized he was in love with her.

She hadn't gotten that at *all.*

Still, even if she had no idea what he was thinking, the compassionate way she was currently gazing at him made him feel vulnerable and uneasy.

"Worse even than the playground was my reaction the first time Matty fell down on the sidewalk and skinned his knee," she continued. "I wasn't sure my heart could take hearing him cry. I felt like the worst mother ever. It took me a long time to realize the best thing to do was not overreact. A character bandage and a kiss is usually sufficient to nurse his little-boy wounds."

"Mmm." It was all Wyatt could do to take her words in, much less give a coherent response.

"Someone once told me that they start growing away from you the moment they're born, and I guess there is some truth to that. Matty gets more independent every day. But I don't have to like it." She chuckled mildly.

"Just enjoy every moment you have with him, I guess," Wyatt agreed, his voice gravelly, thinking about all the times he'd missed.

Carolina made a choking sound. He glanced at her, but she wouldn't meet his eyes.

Was she feeling guilty over all Matty's firsts that she'd denied Wyatt? First breath, first word, the first step Matty took?

He couldn't say as he felt sorry for her. She *should* be feeling guilty. She'd made the decision to walk away. She'd created these consequences for herself, and for Wyatt, and most of all, for Matty.

But today wasn't a day for anger. Today was about spending time with his son.

"Does he like sports?" Wyatt asked.

"Well, I wouldn't say sports, exactly. He's a little young for anything organized yet. Why?"

He felt his face flushing again. He hadn't blushed this much since his senior prom, when he was a gangly youth with two left feet.

"No reason, really. I brought a couple of balls along with me, just in case."

"Oh, now that's a different thing entirely. Matty loves tossing a ball around. Let's see what you've got."

"What do you say, little man?" he asked, scooping Matty into his arms and leading Carolina to his truck. "Do you want to play ball?"

It was only as they reached his truck bed that he realized he'd just set himself up for another round of humiliation and embarrassment. Saying he'd brought a *couple* of balls was a major understatement.

"A couple means two," Matty announced proudly, holding up two fingers. "I'm two."

Wyatt laughed. His kid was super smart, as well as being the cutest boy in the whole state of Texas.

Not that he was biased or anything.

Not knowing what Matty would like, he'd pretty much loaded up every kind of sports ball imaginable—a football, a baseball, a soccer ball and a basketball. He was going to add a couple of baseball gloves, but he only had mitts for adult-size hands. A toddler-size mitt was on his ever-growing list of items he wanted to buy for his son.

Carolina didn't immediately comment when he showed her his stash.

"What? What's wrong?"

"Oh, nothing. We usually play with a big plastic bouncy ball when we're at home."

A bouncy ball.

Another item for his list.

Carolina flashed him half a smile and shrugged apologetically. "I'm afraid I don't know much about these games beyond being able to identify which ball goes with which sport."

"That's what Matty's got a dad for."

He didn't really think about what he was saying until the words had already left his lips.

Their gazes met and locked. She was silently challenging him, but he didn't know about what. Still, he kept his gaze firmly on hers. His words might not have been premeditated, but that didn't make them any less true. He was sorry if he'd hurt her feelings, though. He wanted to keep things friendly between them.

"I think he'd probably enjoy kicking the soccer ball around with you," she said at last.

Whatever antagonism had passed between them was now gone, and he let out the breath he hadn't even realized he'd been holding.

"There's plenty of room on the green for three. What do you say? Do you want to play soccer with us?"

Shock registered in her face, but it was no more than what he was feeling. This was all so new. Untested waters.

Somehow, they had to work things out between the three of them and learn to work together, but kicking a ball around together at the park?

Why, that almost felt as if they were a *family*.

And although in a sense that was technically true, Wyatt didn't even want to go down that road.

He had every intention of being the best father

he could to Matty. And in so doing, he would establish some sort of a working relationship with Carolina, some way they could both be comfortable without it getting awkward. He just couldn't bring himself to think about that right now.

Or maybe he just didn't want to.

After church the next morning, with Matty napping in his car seat, Carolina decided to take a drive out to the countryside to try to clear her head.

Too much was happening, too fast, and she couldn't begin to make sense of it all.

And to think she'd come back to Haven to find some peace and enjoy the slower pace of small-town living. So much for that daydream.

Encountering Wyatt again had changed everything. She'd been in love with him three years ago, and despite the depth of the chasm now between them, she had to acknowledge that she had once been ready to spend her life with him. But he hadn't been ready, and so she'd left. She didn't have any idea if he was ready now, but ready or not, he was a father.

Seeing him kicking the black-and-white ball around with Matty yesterday in the park had shaken her to the core. As far as she was concerned, it was a literal game changer—for all three of them.

Matty needed his father in his life.

Needed Wyatt.

And Wyatt needed him.

She supposed, deep down, she'd always known something was missing during their time in Colorado. As a single mother, she'd often overcompensated as much as she could, attempting to meet all Matty's needs.

But she couldn't be both mother and father to Matty, no matter how she tried. Only Wyatt could truly fill the role of Matty's dad in his life.

Her fists closed tightly around the steering wheel and she huffed out a frustrated breath.

Oh, why did things have to be so complicated? Choices on top of choices, and she wasn't sure any of her decisions, from the day she had walked away until the day she had returned, were right. How was she to judge?

In the best of all possible worlds, Matty wouldn't be the product of a broken home—or rather, a home that never really existed in the first place. But he was.

There were no mom and dad committed to God and each other. No brothers and sisters to play with, no dogs or cats or a family home.

Wyatt was really stepping up as a father, but the cold, hard reality was that even though they would both be in Matty's life—Carolina still wasn't certain to what extent where Wyatt was concerned—they couldn't be with each other. That ship had sailed long ago.

And the worst part was, she had no idea how she was supposed to guard Matty's heart through all of this.

She was going to be in Haven for two months. That meant Wyatt would be a part of Matty's life long enough for their son to get used to the idea of having a father. But what then?

Wyatt's gran would eventually pass on and he would finally be free to follow his dreams, aspirations that would take him far away from Haven and his son.

Matty would be heartbroken. And Carolina wasn't sure how to keep that from happening.

Already she was grieving for what could never be, the family she'd once thought she and Wyatt would eventually make together, however ridiculous the notion was in truth.

This—whatever *this* was—was a whole other thing entirely, and she didn't know what to do with it.

In the quarter hour she'd been driving, she had passed only a handful of drivers on the little-used country road, with miles and miles of Texas prairie on every side of her. Beautiful meadows waving in the wind, with waist-high grass in places.

A beat-up white pickup truck appeared ahead of her, driving well under the speed limit. The driver looked to be an old man, puttering down the highway at the slackened pace of life in the country.

Carolina checked her mirrors and prepared to pass the old codger. Suddenly, the old man slammed on his brakes and the pickup came to an abrupt stop.

Heart in her throat, Carolina swerved to the left, missing the truck by bare inches as the back of her sedan fishtailed and then came to a screeching halt.

Shaken, she pulled her car off to the left shoulder and turned to see if Matty was okay. He was awake but not crying, his startled brown eyes staring straight back at her as he sucked on his fist. Thankfully, his five-point harness had kept him out of harm's way.

"You okay, buddy?" Her voice sounded raspy even to her own ears.

In answer, Matty reached for his sippy cup and self-soothed with his apple juice.

Adrenaline was pulsing so rapidly through Carolina that she couldn't determine whether or not she had any injuries. Her shoulder was a little sore from where the seat belt had locked up, but other than that she thought she'd gotten through the accident without much physical incident.

Her next thought was about the old man who was driving the white pickup.

Why had he stopped so abruptly? Surely he had to have known she would likely rear-end him when he stomped on the brakes the way he had. Had he had some kind of physical breakdown? A heart attack, maybe? Or was he driving under the influence?

He was still sitting behind the wheel of his truck, looking straight down the road, a little dazed. But when Carolina got out of her car to cross the highway to see if he had suffered any injuries or if she needed to call an ambulance, he suddenly gunned his loud, knocking engine and swerved to the left, nearly hitting her as he drove off down the road as fast as the old truck could manage.

All righty, then.

Apparently the man wasn't hurt, although Carolina thought it was very rude of him to drive off without making sure she and her son were okay—especially since it was his fault they'd almost skidded off the road and into a ditch. Some people just didn't have a conscience.

As she returned her gaze to where his truck had been, she discovered the real reason the old man had slammed on his brakes.

A young buck with tiny nubs for antlers lay on its back on the side of the road, its legs twitching as it tried to right itself. Even from where she was standing, she could tell that the poor thing was in trouble.

She didn't want Matty to see it, but she couldn't possibly bring herself to leave the animal to suffer a slow death. She fished her cell phone out of her back pocket, intending to alert the local parks and wildlife station, which was in charge of roadkill in the area.

Except this young buck wasn't roadkill.

Not yet.

Carolina had grown up in the country and knew that often the kindest—if most difficult—thing for a person to do was to put a suffering animal out of its misery, especially a wild animal like this deer. It would never survive out here if it couldn't walk.

Something made her hesitate before making the call to the game department. Maybe it was the way the buck was valiantly, if vainly, struggling to find its feet. Maybe it was the pain and panic clouding its large brown eyes.

Whatever it was, Carolina checked her call log and dialed an entirely different number.

Wyatt's.

He would know what to do, and if it was indeed necessary to put the buck down, he would have the means to give it a quick and painless death. She trusted him to do the right thing for the poor animal.

Relief flooded through her when Wyatt's deep, warm voice answered on the second ring.

"Hey, Carolina. What's up?"

She didn't take time for pleasantries.

"Wyatt, I'm on County Road 8 about fifteen miles out of town. I was taking a Sunday drive when the pickup truck in front of me hit a young buck head-on. I don't know if he wasn't watching where he was going, or if the deer suddenly jumped into the road in front of him. I didn't see it happen. He slammed on his brakes hard and I just barely missed rear-ending him."

"What? Are you okay? Was Matty in the car? Should I call for an ambulance?"

Carolina glanced into the backseat, where Matty had fallen back into a peaceful slumber, and then addressed the issue she imagined was highest on Wyatt's list.

"Matty is in the car with me, but he's fine. I had to swerve and slam on my brakes pretty hard, but Matty is perfectly safe. His five-point car seat straps kept him from experiencing much of a jolt. I'm not sure he even noticed much of a difference from how I usually drive." She laughed unsteadily at her own joke.

"And you?"

"A little shaken up," she admitted. "But physically I'm fine."

"What about the guy driving the truck? Is he okay?" Wyatt's voice tightened.

"He's gone." Carolina couldn't help the note of anger that laced her tone. "He took off without bothering to find out if Matty or I had been injured."

Wyatt made an unintelligible growl from the back of his throat.

"Did you get his license plate number, at least?"

She shook her head, then realized Wyatt couldn't see her movement. "No. But there was really no reason for me to take it. It wasn't exactly an accident. Just a close call."

"Too close. And you're sure you and Matty are all right? No injuries?" he asked again.

"I'm sure. That's not why I'm calling. It's about the buck."

"Do you want me to call the Department of Parks and Wildlife for you?"

"If you think it's best. That's what I was about to do, but then I hesitated and called you instead. I feel kind of silly now. It's just that the buck—he's still moving. I thought maybe…"

Her voice trailed off and then picked up again when she realized how ridiculous she sounded. She was just overemotional from the near accident.

"No. I'm sorry for bothering you. I'm being stupid. I'll call the game warden myself."

"You're not a bother, Carolina. Give me fifteen minutes to find you. And hold off on calling Parks and Wildlife. Maybe there is something I can do."

"You'll come?"

"Of course. I don't know if I can help the buck, but I can at least have a look at him."

"Thank you." She gripped the phone against her chest. Her heart swelled with gratitude. Wyatt had always been that man—the guy who dropped everything to come running when he was needed.

Whether or not he could do anything for the deer, he was making the effort.

She'd called—and he'd answered.

Chapter Five

❦

Wyatt felt sorry for Carolina. Seeing an animal in distress was never a pleasant experience, but to see a deer hit by a truck was especially traumatic. Carolina had a good head on her shoulders and had seen many things as a nurse, but he knew she had a soft spot for animals.

He wished he could help, but he doubted even a man of his expertise could save a wild buck that had been hit by a truck. Some things were beyond him.

That was life. He'd learned not to get too attached to anyone or anything, animals and people alike. At the end of the day, they all went away, leaving a gaping hole where their presence used to be.

His mom and dad hadn't often been there for him as a child, since they were ambassadors in a third-world country and had deemed it not safe for their son. He'd begged and begged to be able to come with them, but they'd refused.

He remembered as a child he would pray every night asking God for his parents' safe return from foreign soil. And what had that gotten him?

They'd been killed. And despite the distance, and not really knowing them very well, Wyatt had felt the void left in his heart.

And he'd never again asked God for anything.

He'd put down more farm animals and domestic pets than he could count, sharing in the family's grief at the loss of a beloved dog or cat but not letting it touch his own heart.

Letting go of people was even harder. As much as he wished it were otherwise, his gran wouldn't be around for much longer. He didn't know what he was going to do without her. She had been everything to him growing up.

Then there were the kids to whom he taught vetting skills at the boys ranch. Despite his effort to stay rational and detached in his volunteer efforts, he couldn't help but become involved, especially with Johnny Drake, the boy he was personally mentoring.

But once again, Wyatt was about to say goodbye. Johnny was seventeen and would be aging out of the program soon, and then he'd be gone, as well.

Worst of all, Wyatt had no guarantee Carolina

would decide to stay in Haven after the party for the seventieth anniversary of the ranch in March.

What if she left and took Matty away?

It would be ridiculously easy for her to throw salt on that old wound and at the same time create a brand-new one by denying him his son.

He *knew* better than to care.

And yet he did.

How could he not? Matty was his son, his flesh and blood. This was one goodbye he was going to fight against.

He spotted Carolina's sedan parked on the opposite shoulder of the road, her car turned the wrong direction from the traffic. Skid marks crossed the road in a fishtail pattern and told the story all on their own.

It could easily have been a lot worse than it had been. The sedan had stopped inches from a two-foot ditch. Wyatt was thankful Carolina and Matty were safe.

He parked his truck a short distance from the buck and walked the rest of the way down the road so as not to frighten the animal further.

Carolina was leaning against the hood of her car, her arms crossed and her cell phone still in her hand. Her glassy eyes were distant as she silently stared at the young buck on the other side of the road, a frown on her lips.

Wyatt's heart went out to her.

Though she must have heard his truck pull up, she didn't appear to realize he was there. He wondered if her physical injuries were worse than she'd first imagined. Or she could be in shock.

He immediately took his denim jacket off and wrapped it around her shoulders. Her gaze shifted to him and her eyes widened.

"Are you okay?" he asked anxiously.

"What do you think?"

"I don't know, Carolina. You don't look so hot right now. Do you want to sit down?"

She chuckled drily. "No. Don't worry about me. What do you think about the buck?"

She nodded toward the yearling, which was still on its side, panting heavily. It was no longer struggling to regain its feet and flee.

"Why don't you sit down so you don't fall down and then let me see if I can get close to it."

"Thank you," she murmured in a scratchy tone.

Wyatt approached the deer slowly, speaking in a low, even tone. "No worries, buddy. I'm a vet. I'm just here to take a look at you, okay?"

He stopped when the buck's eyes rolled white and its nostrils flared. The yearling resumed its bleating and futile kicking motions for a moment, then laid its head back on the ground.

"That's right. No one is going to hurt you."

He crouched by the buck's side and tentatively reached his hand out, running a gentle palm across the deer's flank while he expertly assessed the damage.

The yearling had some deep gashes in its shoulder and flank where it must have made contact with the truck's grille. With all the blood, it was hard to say how deep the wounds were, but Wyatt guessed they were probably not as bad as they looked.

He thought he could clean the gashes against infection and patch up the deer fairly successfully, but he could not oversee its healing if he immediately let the young buck back into the wild. Yet it would never survive without treatment.

His real concern was the deer's legs. If the buck had been physically able, it would have regained its footing on its own and bounded off long ago.

As it was, it almost appeared as if the buck had lost its will to live. And if that was true, nothing Wyatt could do for the deer would help.

"What do you think?" Carolina asked softly. Wyatt hadn't heard her come up behind him. So much for her listening to his directions and sitting down. She was more worried about the deer than she was about herself. She'd always been stubborn that way.

"Can we save the poor thing?"

"Honestly? I don't know. Maybe. I think it depends a lot on how hard this guy wants to fight."

He closely examined the deer's legs but didn't immediately see any cause for alarm. Although he imagined the buck was badly bruised, nothing appeared broken.

"Where's Matty?"

"He's right here."

Wyatt glanced behind him. Matty was clinging to Carolina with one hand and clutched a toy airplane in the other. His dark brown eyes were fastened on the deer.

"Don't get too close, okay, buddy?"

Carolina moved Matty to a spot in the grass and spread out a blanket, well away from the highway and the buck, but close enough that she and Wyatt could both keep an eye on him.

"Is there anything we can do?" Carolina asked, concern lining her tone.

"Let's try to help it onto its feet," he decided. "Be careful to stay away from those hooves and make sure he doesn't try to take a nip at you."

"Okay," she agreed. "What do you need me to do?"

"You support that side of him while I support him under his belly and let's try to roll him up."

Without a second's hesitation, Carolina moved to the opposite side of the deer and carefully stroked the yearling's neck.

"Ready?"

Carolina pressed her lips together and nodded, completely intent on the task ahead of her.

Wild animals were unpredictable at best, and wounded ones even more so. He didn't want to put Carolina in any kind of danger, but he knew her well enough to know he wouldn't be able to talk her out of helping.

For some reason she had her heart set on saving this buck, and incomprehensibly, even to him, that made him want to fight for the animal's life even more, especially when she offered her appreciation once again.

He wouldn't have called it a prayer, but he hoped with his whole heart that when they helped the buck stand up, the injuries wouldn't be as bad as they looked and the deer would find its legs and bound off into the long grass.

It didn't.

Wyatt supported it under its flanks and suspended it steadily on wobbly legs, but as soon as he eased back, the deer's front left leg buckled under it. If Carolina hadn't been on the other side to offer her support, the buck would have plunged down again and would likely have really broken its leg this time.

Together, working without words, they got the yearling safely back down on its side.

"I don't think anything's broken, but it evidently

has a bad sprain, enough that it can't put weight on its leg. It's not going anywhere on its own."

Carolina frowned and her eyes filled with tears. "So there's nothing we can do for him, then."

Her gaze met his, and it was as if she was transferring all her emotions to him through the golden-brown depths of her eyes.

It wasn't just that he could see her anguish and discouragement. He could actually *feel* it.

He cleared his throat and adjusted his Stetson lower over his eyes.

If he was in any other situation, he would have come to the conclusion that the humane thing to do would be to put the suffering animal down.

But when he looked at Carolina's miserable expression, he simply couldn't.

"Let me call Johnny and have him bring us out a trailer. I'm not going to make any promises here, but if we take it back to my ranch I might be able to dress its wounds and wrap its leg."

Carolina let out a deep breath and reached for Wyatt's hand. "Thank you."

He tried to smile encouragingly. "You've said that already. Multiple times, in fact."

"Well, I am grateful. I don't know why this has shaken me up so badly. I am—I *was*—a nurse. It's not like I've never seen blood before, or serious injuries, for that matter."

Wyatt turned her gently by the shoulders and guided her to the blanket where Matty was playing.

"Sit down and try to relax for a few minutes. And please, listen to me this time. You've had quite a scare today, what with almost being in a major car accident. It's no wonder you feel a little unsettled. You're in shock."

And it was clear that she was. Despite the fact that his warm jacket was still wrapped around her, he could feel her shoulders quivering underneath his palms.

He thought she might balk at his suggestion, but she sank onto the blanket with a grateful sigh and offered him an appreciative smile.

He was glad she didn't follow that smile with another thank-you. He didn't know what to do with all her gratitude. It made him antsy and gave him the desire to do even more. He just wasn't certain what more he could do for Carolina.

He scoffed inwardly at his foolishness. It must be some kind of misguided hero complex.

What he *could* do was to take care of the yearling buck. Johnny answered his call on the first ring, and less than a half an hour later, Wyatt, Johnny and Carolina had the frightened deer loaded up in a horse trailer, cushioned by a pile of fresh hay.

"You ought to go home and rest," he urged

Carolina. Her face still appeared pale and her eyes were glassy.

But no, of course she refused to listen to him. Again. Until she saw the young buck completely taken care of, she wasn't going to let this go.

He guessed he really couldn't blame her. He would have done the same thing.

And it wasn't as if he could talk Carolina into or out of anything once she had her mind set on it.

Johnny, mature for his age and always sensitive to the needs of animals, slowly drove the trailer back to Wyatt's ranch. Wyatt followed in his truck, and Carolina brought up the rear in her sedan.

Once they arrived at the ranch and loaded the deer into an empty stall, Wyatt prepared to dress its wounds.

"What do you need me to do?" Carolina asked, coming alongside him and brushing her palms across the denim of her jeans. "Do you have a list of supplies you need?"

"Uh—yes," he answered, caught off guard. He'd expected Johnny to help him vet the buck, since Carolina had their son to worry about. "Where's Matty?"

"Outside playing hide-and-seek with Johnny."

"With *Johnny*?" He couldn't hide his surprise. "How did you manage that? Johnny never interacts with anyone if he doesn't have to."

Carolina raised her eyebrows and shrugged. "How should I know? Maybe small children are his exception. I didn't even have to ask him to help. It was all his idea."

Wyatt ran a hand across the stubble on his jaw. "Hmm. Well, I'll be."

"What? Johnny is reliable, right? We can trust him to watch out for Matty?"

"Absolutely." Wyatt tried to swallow, but his throat had suddenly turned dry. Did Carolina even realize what she'd just said?

She'd said *we*, not *I*.

Whether she consciously admitted it or not, they were in this parenting thing together.

"I figure I'm invested in this animal, so I should do whatever I can to help it," Carolina said, running her palm down the quivering deer's neck. "Now, tell me, what supplies do you need?"

With Carolina's assistance, it took remarkably little time to vet the yearling. She had the same curiously calming influence on the deer as she had on his gran, and Wyatt was able to work quickly to dress the wounds.

After finishing up, they walked outside to find Matty and Johnny.

"Did you and Matty have fun?" Carolina asked as Johnny handed the boy over to her.

"Y-yes, ma'am." Johnny dropped his gaze and his face flared with color.

Carolina put her arm around the teenager and gave him a friendly hug. "Oh, gracious, no, Johnny. Just Carolina is fine. *Ma'am* makes me sound ancient."

To Wyatt's surprise, Johnny lifted his head and offered her a shy smile.

"I l-liked playing with M-Matty."

"That's great to hear. What would you say to doing a little babysitting for me every once in a while? I'm in desperate need of finding people I can trust with Matty."

Johnny's brown eyes grew as wide as his smile. He straightened his shoulders and pushed a curly lock of hair off his forehead.

"I'd really like that, ma'am. C-Carolina," he corrected.

"Wonderful. I'm sure Matty will enjoy spending more time with you."

Johnny nodded vigorously and then turned to Wyatt.

"D-did you invite her and M-Matty to the barn raising next Saturday?"

Heat crept up Wyatt's neck and into his face at Johnny's not-so-subtle attempt at matchmaking.

Matty bobbed his head and reached out for Wyatt. He took his son in his arms, his heart in his throat that Matty wanted to be with him.

Would this ever get old? Would he ever get past

the emotions that rose with the strength of a tidal wave every time he held his son?

"No. I haven't asked her about it yet." It was on the tip of his tongue to say he'd been about to, but really, he hadn't. His mind was too concerned with the right here, right now to worry about next Saturday.

It was a good idea, though. Any extra time he could spend with Matty was a plus. Besides, he wanted to show off his son to the town.

He chuckled. "You beat me to it, Johnny."

Carolina raised an eyebrow. "Are you saying a whole barn needs raising?"

"At the b-boys ranch," Johnny answered before Wyatt could get a word in.

"Someone set fire to one of the barns last month, and members of the Lone Star Cowboy League, along with other volunteers, are building a new one next Saturday. I think some of the ladies in town are also gathering to plan the annual Valentine's Day ice cream social. If that's something that interests you, I'm sure they'd be glad to have you. Would you and Matty like to come?"

Carolina hesitated.

"I understand if you're too busy," he quickly added. Even though he wanted to spend more time with Matty, he didn't want to push Carolina. Not when they were just starting to get along.

Johnny looked crestfallen. Poor kid.

He couldn't blame him. Wyatt was a little down in the mouth about it, as well.

Carolina's gaze swept from Wyatt to Johnny and then back to Wyatt again.

"Too busy? No. It's not that. I'd be happy to help the community if I can. You just caught me off guard, is all. You said someone intentionally burned the barn down? It wasn't an accident?"

"It was ruled an arson by the fire chief," Wyatt said grimly. "There have been more strange things going on as well. When the incidents started, they seemed more like pranks, something a kid would do—letting calves out of their pens, petty theft, just generally creating a ruckus."

He slid his eyes toward Johnny, not wanting to give the teenager the wrong impression. He had every confidence in Johnny and didn't want him to think otherwise.

"At first everyone assumed it was one or more of the resident boys, but now whoever is causing all the problems around the ranch seems to have stepped up his game. Heath Grayson, our local Texas Ranger, now believes the crimes were perpetrated by an adult. And that it's serious business."

"Was anyone hurt in the fire?"

Matty squirmed in Wyatt's arms, and he patted the toddler's back to soothe him. It had been a long, stress-fueled day, and Matty laid his cheek against Wyatt's shoulder. After a minute, the toddler's breath became slow and even.

"No people or livestock were near the barn, thankfully. It was primarily used to store ranch equipment. But I am concerned that the arsonist is still out there somewhere, apparently holding a grudge against the boys ranch."

"That's a frightening thought." Carolina frowned, but when she glanced up at Wyatt, her frown turned into a soft smile. She laid a hand on his arm. "Matty is sound asleep. You've got the touch."

Wyatt grinned, pride welling in his chest. He would much rather not talk about the crimes being perpetrated at the boys ranch while he was enjoying the feel of his son napping in his arms.

He had the daddy touch. Carolina had just said so.

"So you'll c-come?" Johnny asked, gazing at Carolina as if she hung the moon. Wyatt couldn't blame the shy teenager. There was a time not so long ago when Carolina had had the same effect on him.

"Yes," she said, in answer to Johnny's question. But her eyes were on Wyatt. "I'll be there. I'd like the opportunity to participate in Haven community events again."

His breath hitched. Was there a deeper meaning behind her words? Could it be that she was planning to make Haven her permanent home? Would he truly have the opportunity to be a real dad to Matty?

Carolina had broken Wyatt's heart once, and he'd believed it had been beyond mending. Did he dare hope for more than just the promised two months together—or was he setting himself up for a letdown even worse than the first one?

Johnny wandered into the barn to check on the injured buck, and Matty stirred on Wyatt's shoulder.

"Goat?" asked Matty groggily, rubbing his eyes.

Carolina tittered, and Wyatt turned to see what Matty was talking about.

He joined in Carolina's laughter when he saw what Matty was all excited about. One of the baby goats had found a way out of the goat pen and was contentedly munching grass in the middle of Wyatt's yard.

"The escape artist. Guess we're going to have to call that kid Houdini. Matty, would you like to pet the goat?"

"Goat!" Matty exclaimed excitedly, suddenly wide awake.

Suddenly unsure of himself, Wyatt flashed a questioning glance at Carolina. He would keep Matty safe, of course, but he still wanted to make sure she was okay with it.

She smiled and nodded and then knelt by him as he propped Matty on the ground and helped him reach out and pet the black-and-white-spotted baby goat.

"Watch out that he doesn't get his fist clenched in the cute little thing's fur," Carolina warned.

"Gentle, gentle," Wyatt murmured, showing Matty how to run his palm across the animal's coat.

The toddler stayed calm for about two seconds, then squealed and flapped his hands in excitement. The goat balked and bounded away, kicking his legs out behind him as he headed back toward the pen where the rest of the herd was kept.

Matty frowned in disappointment.

"It's okay, sweetheart," Carolina responded tenderly. "Houdini wants to go play with his brothers and sisters now."

Wyatt stood and swung Matty around before handing him back to Carolina. "I'd better make sure our little Houdini gets back in the pen where he belongs and see if I can figure out how he made his escape in the first place."

Carolina rose and brushed off her jeans. "We need to be going anyway."

Wyatt was surprised at the sense of disappointment that swelled in his chest at her words. He had no reason to feel that way. They'd be working together now and he would see Matty often.

He supposed it was just that he'd felt like he'd had a breakthrough with the boy today, that he'd earned the toddler's trust, and Carolina's, as well.

This was just the beginning, he reminded himself. Soon he'd be comfortable being Matty's daddy, and the boy would accept and love Wyatt, as well.

He was amazed at how much his dreams had changed now that he had Matty in his life. He wanted to be where his son was—and he hoped that would be Haven. As honorable as it might have been to do missionary work in foreign countries, Matty's presence here reminded him that he could help people anywhere, even here in Haven. Take Johnny, for example. Surely the classes he held for the boys at the ranch meant something.

And as for Carolina—today had been a good day. Wyatt had been able to help her, and that felt good. She'd needed assistance, and she'd called him.

He didn't want to put too much emphasis on her actions, but he hoped that meant they were building on the tentative trust between them. Because every day he spent with her and Matty brought them closer to the time when she might leave again, this time for good.

Now, more than ever, he realized that he

couldn't handle them going away. He just couldn't. So he would work harder than ever to convince Carolina to stay.

"It's been a good day. How much longer are we going to keep this a secret?" he asked. "About me being Matty's father?"

Her eyes widened, and she captured her bottom lip between her teeth. She looked as if she were vacillating in her mind. Had she not even considered the question?

"I'm sure folks are starting to put two and two together," Carolina said hesitantly. "I don't think we ought to make a big announcement or anything, but if someone asks, I don't see a reason not to tell them the truth."

Wyatt wanted to fist pump. Finally, he could open up about the biggest blessing in his life. Carolina might not want to make a big production out of it, but he wanted to crow the news to the world.

He was Matty's daddy.

Considering that she had zero experience as a receptionist, Carolina settled into her new job at Wyatt's office with surprising efficiency and ease. Her first week of work had gone off without a hitch. It was clear she could use more education in administrative work, but she wasn't intending to make being Wyatt's assistant her permanent occupation. It was the means to an end and nothing more. She wasn't even certain she'd be staying in Haven after the seventieth-anniversary party. Her whole world was still tilted on its axis.

At least Wyatt didn't use a confusing medical filing system. The good old ABCs were satisfactory for his small practice, and as she'd mentioned when he had first offered her employment, the alphabet was a skill she excelled in. Every mother of a toddler did.

And every dad, too, for that matter.

Wyatt had been spending as much time at the office as possible, crouched down on the carpet pushing cars and trucks around and making the motor noise that seemed to be stamped somewhere deep in the male DNA.

He and Matty stacked towers of blocks that Matty delighted in knocking over every bit as much as he enjoyed building them. Wyatt wasn't frustrated by the action. He helped. And he sang endless rounds of children's songs in a deep voice that was as adorably slightly off-key as his son's higher voice was.

Wyatt never lost his patience with Matty, and his enthusiasm was contagious. Carolina couldn't push trucks around for more than five minutes without becoming bored out of her skull, although she forced herself to continue playing as long as Matty liked. She suspected she'd do much better with a daughter's baby dolls and dress up and tea parties.

If she ever had a daughter. It made her sad to think Matty might end up an only child, without brothers and sisters to play with.

Because—maybe especially because—she had been an only child who had longed for siblings, she had always dreamed of having a large family of her own someday.

But then again, she'd never been able to envision sharing her life with anyone but Wyatt. No other man had ever measured up.

And Wyatt had had other plans. Or at least she'd thought he'd had. Now she wasn't certain about anything.

Even with as much joy as she experienced, it had been a long, awkward and sometimes painful week, watching Wyatt on the floor with his son, laughing and playing with Matty just as she'd always imagined he would do. She'd always known that when and if he ever reached that point in his life, Wyatt would be a wonderful father.

And he was. A natural.

But this wasn't how it was supposed to be.

Not knowing for sure if she was dressing for a barn raising or if she would be helping to plan a social event, Carolina dressed in layers, a lilac velour pullover over a T-shirt, an older pair of blue jeans and the comfortable cowboy boots that were now part of her daily ensemble.

It wasn't like her to fuss over an outfit. Scrubs had been her go-to clothes for many years, and there wasn't anything fancy about those. But for some reason, today she hesitated before the full-length mirror attached to her bathroom door and gave herself a critical once-over.

She clicked her tongue against her teeth and scoffed. She wasn't trying to impress Wyatt—er—*anybody*. So why had his face, and his expression as she remembered it from when they were dating, shining with admiration and affection, instantly flashed through her mind?

That wasn't simply a little harmless daydream. It was a full-blown disaster in the making. It was next to impossible not to linger on past emotions, which somehow were now starting to feel more immediate and current.

And strong. Oh, so strong.

Confusion rolled through her in waves as she struggled to tuck and file her emotions away, out of sight and mind.

Lately—as in ever since she'd come back to Haven—it seemed she had to remind herself over and over again that her life was now centered around Matty and Matty alone. No good could come from throwing bygone feelings from her past with Wyatt into what was already a precipitous situation.

Determined to shove those emotions aside, she was buckling Matty into his car seat when she noticed the red flag on her pillar mailbox was raised.

Now, that was odd. She knew she hadn't used the box for any letters to be mailed. Was someone else using her mailbox for some reason?

Curious, she opened the door to the metal mailbox and peered inside. Sure enough, there was a letter, but it wasn't outgoing as one would expect, given that the flag was up.

Instead, she found an envelope addressed to her in an unsteady script of black ink.

Clearly it hadn't come through the official postal system. For one thing, the regular mailman didn't put the flag up when he delivered the mail—he put it down after taking any letters she intended to mail out.

Just as telling, the envelope she now held in her hand was not only devoid of a return address, but a stamp, as well.

Still, it *was* her name on the envelope.

She slid behind the wheel of her sedan, glanced in the rearview mirror to make sure Matty was happily amusing himself and used her index finger to break the seal of the envelope. She pulled out a single sheet of lined notebook paper, which had been folded at odd angles in order for it to fit into the greeting-card-size envelope.

She chewed on her bottom lip as she read the strange missive.

Deer Carolina,
Will you please go to the ice cream social with me?
    If yes, meat me there and wear red.
Your valentine,
Wyatt

What on earth?

She couldn't help it. She started giggling, and once she began, she couldn't seem to stop, not until she had tears running down her face. Maybe it was all the stress she'd been facing, or possibly a lack of sleep, but all of her emotions came pouring out in her laughter.

"Mama?" Matty was clearly concerned that his mother had completely lost her wits, but he was also laughing right along with her.

Or possibly *at* her.

She snorted and tried to gather her composure.

"I'm fine, honey. It's just that I'm reading a funny letter."

Funny letter, indeed.

And her response?

Even worse.

Because despite the fact that the mysterious missive had arrived in her mailbox without a stamp, sporting an unsteady script and riddled with more questions than answers—not to mention a couple of spectacular spelling errors that nearly set her off giggling again—her very first response had come from her heart.

Yes, she would wear red.

Yes, she would be Wyatt's valentine.

If it was really Wyatt asking. But of course, this was all stuff and nonsense, possibly even someone's idea of a cruel joke.

She hadn't a clue who would go through all the effort of creating and delivering a fake invitation, or why they would bother with her, since she had just arrived back in town.

Most of all, she couldn't imagine why they had signed Wyatt's name at the bottom.

Wyatt, of all people.

Someone certainly had their wires crossed.

She dabbed at the corner of her eyes and tossed the letter into her handbag on the passenger seat.

She was already running late because she'd taken too much time in front of the mirror. Now, having been waylaid by this silly invitation, it would be all she could do to make the official 8:00 a.m. starting time. With it being a community event, she suspected parking was going to be a bear.

She was right about that. Trucks lined the driveway from the entrance to the boys ranch onward, and some vehicles were even parked on both sides of the street that bordered the property.

Not wanting to walk a long distance with a toddler in tow, Carolina picked her way toward the main house, hoping she could find a spot that hadn't yet been taken. Her sedan was considerably smaller than most of the ranchers' trucks, and thankfully she was able to find an open location near the front of the house.

Katie Ellis met her as she was plucking a wiggling Matty out of his car seat.

"Carolina. I'm glad you could make it today. This is going to be so much fun with you here."

Carolina handed Matty off into Katie's waiting arms while she gathered the toddler's play belt and tools, which he had somehow managed to spread out all over the backseat of the car in the fifteen minutes it had taken them to get from Uncle Mort's cabin to the boys ranch. Add to that five minutes to find parking, she mentally amended.

For an active toddler like Matty, that was more than enough time to make a complete mess out of his toys, and it took her a minute to find and arrange the little plastic hammer, saw and screwdriver, as well as a jumble of other tools, onto the pint-size tool belt.

"How adorable," Katie admired as Carolina wrapped the tool belt around Matty's waist. "He'll fit right in with all the other builders."

"Right? Wyatt got this set for him."

"Daddy-son day?" Because of all the friendship and support Katie had lent her, she was one of the few to whom Carolina had admitted the truth about Wyatt and Matty.

Carolina nodded and tried to smile, though her heart dipped. Katie's words had taken her by surprise, that's all.

"Speaking of which—have you seen Wyatt? I'm not sure what Matty and I are supposed to be doing today."

"He's right—"

"Behind you," Wyatt finished for her, his voice a low rumble that simultaneously sent a skitter of electric recognition across Carolina's nerves and yet soothed something deep in her chest.

Wyatt stepped up next to her and took Matty from Katie's arms. Carolina swallowed through a dry throat, feeling his presence as if he had touched her, even though he stood several inches away.

Apparently her personal space expanded when she was around Wyatt.

"I'll take Matty with me to the building site. Johnny is going to be with me all day to help keep an eye on Matty so he doesn't get into any trouble."

Was it Carolina's imagination, or did Wyatt sound a little bit defensive?

She couldn't help but think *she* was the one who was in trouble, but of course she didn't say so. She wasn't handling this so well, emotionally speaking.

"We'll see you men at lunch." Katie threaded her arm through Carolina's and flashed Wyatt a shy smile.

This had all happened so fast that Carolina's head was reeling, but she allowed Katie to lead her into the main entrance of the boys ranch while Wyatt walked away with Matty in his arms.

"A bunch of us ladies are meeting in the dining room to plan the ice cream social," Katie explained. "We need to settle on a theme and some ideas for decorations. Lila's Café always caters the event, so we don't have to worry about hors d'oeuvres or punch."

Bea Brewster led the meeting. Carolina recognized many familiar faces. She privately admitted she'd dragged her feet in attending, wondering if people were going to judge her for the choices she'd made, coming back to town as a single mother.

But if anyone thought that way, they certainly didn't show it. Every woman in the group welcomed her openly and asked for her opinions.

When the meeting broke an hour later, plans had been set in motion for the Lady in Red–themed ice cream social. Carolina had volunteered for the decorating committee, and they had also been in charge of developing the overall idea for the social.

The theme had been Carolina's idea—or rather, it had come to her through the strange note she'd received earlier in the day. She thought it was rather clever, but only because she had no intention of being there herself, much less wearing red to the event.

She wouldn't want to give whoever had written the puzzling invitation the wrong impression about her and Wyatt.

"Whatever you were just thinking about, you have to share. Do you have a hot date for the Valentine's social?"

Carolina choked on her breath. She was glad she hadn't been sipping coffee from the mug in front of her or the hot liquid would have gone down the wrong pipe and she would have spit it halfway across the room. As it was, she couldn't catch her breath.

"Gracious, no," she managed to rasp.

Katie arched her blond eyebrows and her green

eyes sparkled impishly. "I thought maybe Wyatt would have asked you."

"Absolutely not," Carolina assured her. "Wyatt and I are a thing of the past. We share a child. That's as far as it goes. He barely tolerates me, and trust me, that is only for Matty's sake."

"Is that what you think?"

"Why? Has he said something?" Her rebellious heart leaped into double time.

"No," Katie was quick to amend. "But I've seen the way he looks at you when he thinks no one is watching him. I'm good at reading other people's expressions."

"I'm sure you are, but this time you're mistaken."

Katie chuckled. "Am I?"

Carolina nodded, but the thought, even if it was erroneous, made her chest cloud with a half dozen unnamed and undesired emotions.

Whatever Wyatt thought about her, it wasn't in any way romantic. Of that much she was certain. But there was something she wanted to ask, and Katie was the perfect person to provide an answer while at the same time being discreet about it.

She dug into her handbag and withdrew the questionable invitation. "I did receive this. And to be honest, I'm completely flummoxed by it."

She slid the envelope over to Katie, who quickly

scanned the contents and then promptly burst into laughter.

Carolina grinned. "Isn't that the funniest thing you've ever seen? Those spelling mistakes are to die for. It's obviously not from Wyatt."

"Obviously," Katie agreed, clearly trying to maintain her composure.

"It just randomly showed up in my mailbox this morning. No stamp or return address. Whoever stuck it in there put the flag up so I would notice. I'm assuming this is some kind of prank, but what I can't figure out is who would do this and why anyone would sign Wyatt's name to it."

"The mystery matchmakers."

"The what who?"

"They've been wreaking a bit of havoc all over town for the last few months now. No one has yet discovered who they are, although many of us suspect it may be some of the more impish residents of the boys ranch. It sounds like they are really stepping up their game for Valentine's Day. I've heard of a lot of missives being delivered. It's one of the perks of being the boys ranch secretary. I hear all the gossip."

"Fill me in."

"It's kind of cute, really. And whoever they are, they've been remarkably accurate in their predictions. Couples are coming together thanks to them. They've had quite a few more wins than losses."

"Score this one in the loss column," Carolina assured her with a laugh.

"You should wear red to the social." Again, the gleam in Katie's eyes was unmistakable.

Carolina fidgeted in her seat.

"I'm certainly not going to encourage them—whoever *they* are, with their silly matchmaking scheme. I can't imagine why they would bother with me, and I don't want them thinking Wyatt and I are an item." She paused. "What about you? Who have these mystery matchmakers paired you with?"

Katie shook her head and smiled weakly. "I'm apparently flying under their radar."

Carolina thought she heard a note of melancholy in her tone and was going to ask about it, but Katie continued before she could say a word.

"That's just as well. Really. I'm already head over heels in love with someone, although he doesn't even know I exist. There's no hope for me, and I don't think the mystery matchmakers could help."

"Who is it?" Carolina felt a little as if she were back in high school again, gossiping with a good friend. It was a light, happy feeling, and she hadn't had too many of those lately, so she embraced it.

It was much better than worrying about her own problems. It was refreshing to think about someone else's relationship status for a change, even if poor Katie seemed to be having her share of problems in the romance department.

Katie leaned in so only Carolina could hear her speak. "Can you keep a secret?" she whispered.

"Of course." Carolina's grin widened and she made a motion of locking her lips and throwing away the key.

"It's Pastor Andrew." Katie sighed dramatically. "I'm pretty sure he doesn't even know I exist, other than being one of his most devoted parishioners. I don't miss a service." Her brow scrunched over her nose and she giggled. "Oh, dear. That doesn't sound very good, does it? I really do go to church to worship God. But I can't help how I feel about Pastor Andrew. The heart wants what the heart wants, as they say. Oh, well. It's not like I would be a good minister's wife."

"I don't know about what *they* say, but I say if Pastor Andrew hasn't noticed you, then he's the one who is missing the mark. If you ask me, he ought to get his eyes checked and his head examined. You're a beautiful woman, inside and out. A man would be crazy not to notice you."

Katie's cheeks turned a pretty shade of pink. "You know what? Don't worry overmuch about keeping my secret." She highlighted the word *se-*

cret in air quotes. "I'm fairly certain everyone in Haven knows I'm pining after the minister. Everyone except him, that is."

"Let's see what we can do about that." Carolina was already formulating possibilities in her mind to help her friend get the pastor's attention.

Katie squeaked and laid a hand on Carolina's forearm. "No. Please don't. I'd die of embarrassment."

She laughed. "Don't worry. I was just kidding. I wouldn't want to interfere in anyone's love life. Trust me. My own track record in the romance department is a dismal failure. It wouldn't be wise of you to take any advice from me."

"Maybe we'll both find someone special at the ice cream social," Katie suggested, although her tone indicated she didn't really believe what she was saying.

"That could be problematic, since I'm not going to be there."

"What?" Katie squawked, sounding a bit like a macaw. "Oh, yes, you are. Please say you are *not* going to leave me alone as the only wallflower in the room."

"Somehow I don't think you'll be alone for long. You couldn't possibly be a wallflower."

"I will be if you aren't there to offer moral support. The whole night will be a complete disaster."

Carolina narrowed her gaze thoughtfully. "Is Pastor Andrew going to be there?"

Katie laughed. "I'm sure he will be. He never misses an opportunity to eat free food."

Carolina knew she was going to regret what she was about to say next. She had no desire to be, as Katie had called it, a wallflower at this event.

Even worse, someone out there thought she and Wyatt still belonged together, enough to take the time to write a note. What if these mystery matchmakers somehow tried to push them together at the social?

Maybe Wyatt wouldn't show up at the social at all. She could hope, couldn't she?

Because she could hardly say no to Katie's request, not when the young woman had been such a big help to her since she'd come back to town, lending an ear when Carolina needed to talk and watching Matty whenever she needed assistance or had a job interview.

Matty.

He might just be her ticket out.

Everyone in town would be at the social— Katie included. Which would mean finding Matty a babysitter would be next to impossible.

"I'll come with you," she agreed with a shrug, "as long as I can find someone to watch Matty.

Although at this late date I doubt I'll be able to find anyone suitable."

Katie squealed in delight. "Yay! It's a done deal, then. You probably didn't know this, but child care will be provided right here at the social."

Carolina groaned inwardly.

What had she just been talked into? Nothing she wanted to do, that was for sure. She would have tried to find another excuse to back out, but Katie's expression looked so hopeful, flooding with joy.

Apparently, Carolina was going to the Lone Star Cowboy League's Valentine's Day ice cream social.

But she would not—*not*—wear red.

Chapter Six

Wyatt couldn't remember a day when he had ever had as much fun as he was having at this moment. Who knew that having a child—*his* child—accompany him to a community event could bring such a ray of sunshine into his life?

He'd always wanted to be a father, but it had seemed like a distant dream, especially after Carolina had disappeared from his life. To have Matty with him now seemed like more of a blessing than he deserved.

But he would take it, and be grateful for it.

Wyatt's chest burst with pride for his little guy, who, with Johnny's gentle, constant assistance, fastidiously mimicked his daddy's every move, using his little plastic tools to saw and hammer the random chunks of two-by-fours Wyatt had provided for him.

Johnny's attention was focused far more on

Matty than on the construction going on around them. Wyatt couldn't have asked for better help.

He grinned at the pair. They almost looked like brothers with their heads together, animatedly working on their little project. Wyatt was still amazed at how much Johnny had come out of his shell with Matty. The teenager's stutter wasn't as pronounced when he was around the toddler, and they looked equally excited about the little house they were making from wood scraps and some glue.

Wyatt stopped and watched them for a minute. There was something about being responsible for the welfare of his dark-haired little boy that spoke to the deepest, most protective and masculine part of Wyatt's heart. His feelings for Matty opened up a whole new world for him.

He might have missed a couple of Matty's formative years, but he was here now, and here he intended to stay.

"I can't believe how much you guys have already done on the barn."

Carolina had approached from behind him and he hadn't seen her coming, but he turned and smiled at her.

"We have plenty of help here today. It should be no problem finishing before the sun goes down."

"I hope Matty wasn't underfoot too much for you. I was worried he might get in the way."

"Not at all. You'll be happy to know that our son is a regular builder," Wyatt said, showing off the little house Matty and Johnny had constructed. He couldn't help the way his chest swelled with pride.

"How cute," Carolina exclaimed, stooping down to admire the project. "What a neat-looking house. It has a door and windows, too. Very clever."

"That was M-Matty's idea," Johnny said, pushing his hair off his forehead.

"Well, it looks to me like you've been a big help to him. I'm sure he couldn't have done it without you."

Wyatt could see how much her compliment meant to the teenager, and the smile she flashed him had the young man grinning ear to ear. It was good to see Johnny happy. He didn't smile very often.

But it wasn't Johnny's smile that had Wyatt uncomfortably shifting his weight. When Carolina's countenance warmed, Wyatt's nerves energized and his pulse leaped. Suddenly he was having difficulty finding his voice.

After everything he and Carolina had been through, after her heartless betrayal of everything Wyatt held dear, how could her smile—and worse yet, one that was not even directed at him—make him feel giddy and light-headed?

He wondered what would happen if she looked at *him* with such happiness and joy in her eyes.

No. He did not.

Been there. Done that. Ripped up and threw away the T-shirt.

How many times did he need to remind himself that whatever feelings she evoked in him didn't count?

He sighed inwardly. He'd probably have to keep mentally giving himself the same warning until he no longer felt anything when he looked at Carolina.

Which was likely to be never.

He shook his head. There was undeniable chemistry between them. Nothing more. As long as he knew it was only the sound of her laughter and the floral scent of her perfume that was jogging his memories, he could keep a handle on it, remain in control.

And he would keep telling himself that until he believed it.

Carolina scooped Matty into her arms and swung him around until he giggled with delight. Up until that moment, Wyatt would never have imagined that a mother holding a child could be attractive to a man, but there was no doubt about it when his heart flooded with emotions.

The protectiveness and affection he felt couldn't

be denied or written off, nor could the fact that it wasn't only Matty who precipitated those feelings.

No.

This had to stop. Right now.

He turned his gaze away from Carolina and picked up his hammer.

"I came to tell you lunch is ready." If she noticed his sudden aversion to her, she didn't react to it. "We're serving sandwiches buffet style in the backyard. We borrowed fold-up tables from the church for the meal."

Wyatt's stomach rumbled and Carolina laughed.

He frowned.

Stupid stomach.

Even his gut unrepentantly responded to her voice.

Nothing but trouble, Harrow.

But he *was* hungry, so he reluctantly joined Carolina, Matty and Johnny as they walked back to the main house. Carolina kept up a lively conversation, asking Johnny about school, his veterinary work with Wyatt and how the young buck they had saved from the middle of the road was faring.

The young man's stutter increased when he spoke to her, but he seemed happy to have her attention. He stayed close even after they'd piled up their plates full of food, even though most of the other boys were already seated. Wyatt felt bad for Johnny, but Matty was pleased by the teenager's presence, and Johnny didn't seem to mind.

Wyatt could only pick out bits and pieces of the chatter, but not surprisingly, the topic of the day appeared to be the backlash the boys ranch was feeling due to the arson and thefts.

"Why do I feel as if there is more of a problem here than just the burned-down barn?" Carolina asked, sliding onto a chair opposite Wyatt, balancing Matty in one arm and two plates of food in the other. She set Matty down next to her and passed him one plate.

"The Department of Family and Protective Services has recently been taking a good, hard look at the boys ranch," he explained.

Bea Brewster took a seat next to Wyatt, and Katie sat down next to Carolina.

"We're afraid the DFPS is going to show up here unannounced," said Bea, clicking her tongue. "We're running this ranch completely by the book, of course, but you know how it is. If they're actively looking for some broken regulation, they'll probably find one. None of us is perfect."

"We'd just as soon get completely off their radar," Katie added. "And sooner rather than later."

Wyatt couldn't help but notice how Katie's gaze kept straying toward Pastor Andrew. When the pastor waved in her direction, her cheeks turned pink and she quickly looked away.

Poor woman. Unrequited love was the worst. He should know.

"As if we needed the extra stress." Darcy Hill, along with her fiancé, Nick, joined the small group. Only recently engaged, they should have only had eyes for each other, but Wyatt could see the strain on their faces from all of the current stress. "We're having a hard enough time working out all the details of the seventieth-anniversary party. Between Gabe not being able to find his grandfather and us not having any success locating the real Avery Culpepper so she can claim her part of the will—well, let's just say things could be better."

Nick kissed Darcy's temple. "Trust in the Lord and He will direct your path," he paraphrased, his voice not a reprimand but a gentle reminder.

"I know. I know. I think I've narrowed our viable choices down to one woman, but she lives in Tennessee and won't respond to my calls and letters. Still, it looks promising. Her mother's name was Elizabeth and her birthday is February second. The facts fit together. I only wish I could get a personal confirmation from her."

"Maybe try to connect with her through social media?" Carolina suggested.

Darcy smiled, her expression full of determination. "I tried that, too, but so far I haven't heard back. Otherwise I may have to fly out to Tennessee and hunt her down in person. This reunion is far too important to the future of the boys ranch, and too many people have worked too hard on it, for us to fail now."

"Hear, hear," said Wyatt, toasting his cola can at her. He wished he could personally do more to make sure the seventieth-anniversary party went off without a hitch, but there was little he could do to help.

What he *could* do was make sure he crossed all his t's and dotted all his i's where the boys ranch animal programs were concerned. The DFPS, if they did happen to show up unannounced, would find all the ranch animals in excellent condition and his program running precisely by the book.

"Gabe's grandfather is estranged from his family?" Carolina asked no one in particular.

"Theodore Linley is not only estranged," Nick answered, running a hand through his chestnut-brown hair, "but he has vanished right off the globe. It's kind of sad, really. He abandoned his family when Gabe was about eight, and he was in prison for a while on charges of petty theft, but no one has heard from him since. The prison is officially his last known whereabouts. After he was released, he just disappeared. I don't think he wants to be found."

Wyatt cringed inwardly. He felt sorry for Gabe. If ever a man needed divine assistance, it was Gabe. This situation definitely warranted it. So many people depended on one man's success.

Wyatt's thoughts were almost a prayer.

Almost.

Feeling uncomfortable in his own skin, Wyatt broke a freshly baked chocolate chip cookie in half and showed it to Carolina.

"Is it okay for Matty to have a cookie?"

"Cookie!" Matty exclaimed.

"Oops." Wyatt grinned awkwardly.

Carolina chuckled. "No worries. He was a good boy and ate all of his sandwich. I don't think half a cookie will do him any harm. I'll make sure he brushes his teeth as soon as we get back to the cabin."

As Wyatt offered his son the cookie, a ruckus broke out near the end of the table. Wyatt glanced up to see two of the boys ranch residents—blond-haired, blue-eyed Danny McCann and brown-haired, blue-eyed Jasper Boswell—giggling and shoving each other. They were both eight years old, and they both had similar impish expressions on their faces. They were obviously looking for trouble.

Danny carried a single pink rose with a note tied to it—a sheet of typing paper folded into quarters. The laughing boys made a lunge toward Katie

Ellis, whose face had gone from pink to a flaming red as Danny thrust the rose toward her and she took the bloom in her hand.

"Oh, my," she breathed, and then giggled in delight. "This is for me?"

"Flying under their radar, huh?" Carolina teased, nudging Katie with her shoulder.

Wyatt fought to restrain a grin. He didn't have to ask who *they* were. The mystery matchmakers had struck again. And Katie seemed happy to be the recipient.

Odd, though, that the boys were delivering the message in person, in a public place, right out in the open where everyone could see. Up until now the matchmakers had acted in private, not revealing their identities as they slyly delivered their messages.

Like, for example, the note he had found on the welcome mat on his front porch just this morning. Short, sweet and to the point.

Carolina would be waiting for him at the ice cream social. And she would be wearing red.

He knew very well the note hadn't been from Carolina, and he hadn't even stopped to consider why the mystery matchmakers would choose her as his date in the first place.

So it was Jasper Boswell and Danny McCann playing Cupid, was it? Wyatt couldn't say he was completely surprised, although the fact that they were only eight years old seemed a little strange. How could such young boys manage to pull off these stunts?

Could they even write the kinds of notes folks were getting? And what did eight-year-old boys know about romance? Whoever the mystery matchmakers were had been surprisingly accurate in their pairings. He suspected some of the older boys were involved, as well, if for nothing else because someone needed to drive the younger kids around.

Conversation ceased as Katie unfolded the note and scanned its contents.

Her smile dropped from her face and tears sprang to her eyes. She stood so abruptly her silverware clattered.

"Excuse me," she said, her hand flying to her throat as she ran into the house.

Carolina's distressed gaze met Wyatt's and he arched his brow in question. Carolina had been close enough to be able to read the note. What was written on it that had sent poor Katie running off in tears?

Carolina shook her head with a brief jerk of her chin and mouthed the word *later*.

"Keep an eye on Matty?" she asked aloud.

"Of course." No question there.

Carolina took off after Katie and Wyatt switched sides of the table so he was sitting next to his son.

"Is K-Katie going to be all right?" Johnny asked. Wyatt knew Katie was one of the few people who was always kind to Johnny, so he wasn't surprised that the teenager was concerned about her.

"Oh, I imagine she'll be fine," Wyatt answered with what he hoped was a reassuring grin. "It's just girl stuff. You know how women can be. Katie's probably in the bathroom crying because she is so happy to have received a rose."

Johnny didn't look convinced. Probably because Wyatt wasn't, either.

But whatever the note had said, and whatever Katie's reaction had truly been to its contents, she was blessed to have a friend like Carolina. For all her faults, Carolina was the compassionate shoulder Katie could cry on—happy, sad or somewhere in between.

He wasn't going to be in the office much the following week, but he figured he would find out the details eventually. If not, he'd ask about Katie, make sure she was okay.

If he had to guess, he would think the note had something to do with the Valentine's social. He imagined both Carolina and Katie would be there—as, much to his dismay, would he.

As a general rule, he didn't care for dances, but he had promised to escort Gran to the event. The elderly population of Haven's nursing home would stay for the first hour to enjoy the party and then be taken back to the home by orderlies. Wyatt hoped it would do Gran good to attend a social outing, although of course that was never a sure thing, especially lately.

In the meantime, if he found the opportunity to do so, he thought he might have to have a word with Danny and Jasper. A harmless prank was one thing, but making a woman cry? That was something else entirely. If they had anything to do with it, Wyatt would see that they apologized to poor Katie.

He wondered which, if any, of the other boys were involved in the mystery matchmaking she-nanigans. He briefly considered telling the boys about his own letter, but then thought better of it.

If Danny and Jasper weren't the only ones writing these notes—and Wyatt's gut told him that they weren't—then he didn't want to draw their attention to his supposed match with Carolina. That was inconsequential information.

Even if it had somehow left an indelible mark in Wyatt's heart.

The attempted matchmaking would eventually blow over on its own—although for his sake, and for Carolina's, he hoped she wouldn't be wearing red at the Valentine's social.

That could be bad.

Very bad, indeed.

* * *

Carolina stood in a corner on the far side of the church's fellowship hall, which she had helped transform into a Valentine's Day wonderland of red, pink and glittering silver hearts, bows and ribbons.

The silk blouse she was wearing was the only thing in her closet that even remotely resembled anything that would work for a Valentine's Day party. With her complexion, she couldn't pull off most shades of pink, and she hadn't had time to go shopping for anything a little less blatantly—

Red.

She'd only agreed to wear the telling color because it was part of the overall theme and she didn't want to let Katie down, not to mention the ladies who'd planned the event. She didn't want to inadvertently offend anyone.

So, limited in her choices, she had arrived in traditional Valentine's Day colors.

The Lady in Red.

Yep. That was her.

She wanted to roll her eyes. After only half an hour, she was already turning herself into the most modern definition of the word *wallflower*, and she was grateful she wasn't standing out from the crowd by wearing blue or green.

Which she had considered.

But *why* did it have to be red?

She felt as if dozens of eyes were surreptitiously upon her—she who had exactly followed the instructions of the mystery matchmakers. Were they gleefully giggling somewhere?

Not that anyone other than the kids who wrote the note—and Katie, who'd read it—would even know what was contained within. But the last thing she wanted to do was inadvertently encourage silly boys' misconceptions.

What if they left a note for Wyatt next time?

A shock of adrenaline bolted through her as it occurred to her that Wyatt might already have received a similar missive.

What if he would be looking to see if she wore red?

After that first moment of alarm, she calmed down. He hadn't said anything about having received a letter, so she was probably safe.

Katie had insisted that she and Carolina park themselves in the corner nearest the ice cream sundae bar, since dessert would presumably be the utmost thought in most of the single men's minds.

Single men, meaning Pastor Andrew, Carolina thought, amused. She didn't want to mention that she had no interest whatsoever in the single men of Haven.

At first, Katie had been taken aback and was downright indignant by the mystery matchmakers' note. With as deep as Katie's feelings ran, it was hardly a joking matter to tease her with a letter.

Unlike Carolina's awkwardly scribbled note, Katie's had been carefully typewritten. Even the signature was typeset.

Be my valentine at the ice cream social.
Pastor Andrew

Katie had regained her composure shortly after receiving the note and the rose, and, in her usually upbeat way, had overcome her initial sensitivity.

A typed signature? That was a dead giveaway for sure. There was no sense in her being a bad sport when most of the other singles in town had also received letters.

Carolina hoped Pastor Andrew hadn't heard about it. It seemed to her that the minister was as shy and awkward around Katie as she was with him. Knowing there had been an attempt at matching up the two would only serve to make things worse for both of them.

Along with Katie, Carolina was keeping her eyes trained on the door, watching laughing couples enter and mingle, and silently praying that someday, one of those happy couples would be Katie and Pastor Andrew.

A tiny flame flickered in her heart—one that she barely dared acknowledge.

The hope that she might one day have someone special to share her life with.

Her pulse jumped when Wyatt entered the room, gently escorting his gran through the crowd and to a chair near where some of her friends from the nursing home were located.

Katie nudged Carolina's shoulder with hers. "What are you waiting for? For Wyatt to notice your red blouse?"

"Ha-ha. Very funny."

Carolina was not amused.

But she did want to go speak to Eva. It was sweet of Wyatt to bring his grandmother to the social. If Eva was having a lucid day, she would welcome Carolina's familiar face. If not, Wyatt could more than likely use all the help he could get to keep her happy.

Either way...

"All right. But you're coming with me." Carolina looped her arm through Katie's, ignoring the heat rising to her face. She felt like a teenager at her first high school dance.

It wasn't a fond memory.

Eva, she reminded herself. She was doing this for Eva. There was no reason for her to feel uncomfortable.

"Eva," Carolina exclaimed as they neared. "I

see you managed to talk your handsome grandson into being your date for the dance."

The older woman's eyes met hers and flashed with recognition.

"Carolina."

She crouched before the old woman and took both of her hands. Her skin felt thin and brittle to the touch, like parchment paper.

"Wyatt?"

"I'm here, Gran."

Wyatt shifted so his grandmother could see him, standing directly behind Carolina. His warm palm brushed her hair off her shoulder and electricity skittered down her spine.

Eva clucked at them. "Wyatt, take your wife out there and dance. I'll be fine here for a little while."

Carolina scrambled to make sense of the words, and it took her a while to realize Eva's gaze was resting firmly on her.

"I'm not—"

"You know I don't dance." Wyatt's laugh sounded forced as he squeezed Carolina's shoulder.

A silent reminder.

Of course. She was the registered nurse here, and yet she'd been the one to get confused. She, more than anyone, ought to know that Eva's faculties weren't working at full capacity. Her mind worked in bits and pieces. Eva probably remembered her and Wyatt together in the past and, seeing them together now, had mistakenly made more of it than it was.

Much more.

And she was embarrassed to realize how completely that connection had thrown her off.

Wyatt had done the right thing—redirecting his grandmother without correcting her misconceptions. In a short time, Eva wouldn't remember what she had said, anyway.

But Carolina would.

Eva's statement would be branded on her mind for a long time to come.

Carolina stood abruptly, her shoulders plowing into Wyatt's chest. He put out his hands to steady her.

"I'm sorry, I—" She searched for an excuse to make a speedy exit, but nothing came to mind.

She was grateful when Katie stepped in.

"Carolina and I were about to get a bowl of ice cream," Katie said cheerfully. "Wyatt, can we get you and your gran anything? A glass of punch or something?"

Wyatt shook his head, and Carolina scrambled back to the safety of the corner wall she'd originally been holding up, leaning against it and focusing on slowing her breath.

She would never, *ever* complain about being a wallflower again.

"Well, that was interesting," Katie said with a laugh. "Mrs. Harrow."

Carolina groaned. "Please. Let's not even go there."

She needn't have worried. A moment later, Katie grabbed Carolina by the shoulders and ducked behind her.

"What now?"

"I'm so not ready for this."

Carolina spotted Pastor Andrew in the crowd and had to remind herself that Katie was still a young woman, with a young woman's hopes and dreams. It couldn't be easy for her, crushing on the town's minister—

Who looked like he was walking straight toward them.

"Katie, I think you'd better—" Carolina started to warn, but she didn't have the opportunity to complete her statement before Pastor Andrew was upon them.

He was a tall, lanky man with kind hazel eyes. He scrubbed a hand through his light brown hair as he approached.

He looked as nervous as Katie was acting. Katie made an incomprehensible squeaking sound but stepped forward, smoothing her bright pink dress with her hand.

"Katie," Pastor Andrew said, and then, almost as an afterthought, he nodded at her. "Carolina."

Carolina didn't mind at all that the minister only had eyes for the boys ranch secretary. This could be good. She sent up a silent prayer for the couple.

Pastor Andrew cleared his throat and shoved his hands into the pockets of his black slacks. He had a real gift in the pulpit and in counseling the boys at the ranch, but he looked like he was having trouble speaking to Katie. His Adam's apple bobbed and he cleared his throat a second time.

"Katie, I—I was just… How are you?"

Somehow Carolina didn't think that was the question the minister had intended to ask, but Katie, her face taking on a rosy glow that matched the color of her dress, didn't seem to notice.

"Very well, thank you," she answered shyly. "And you?"

"I'm good. Fine. That is, I just—" Pastor Andrew hesitated and rocked back on the heels of his cowboy boots. He took a deep breath and let it all out at once in a string of words. "Here's the thing. I was wondering if you read my note."

Katie's eyes went as wide as saucers. Carolina had to admit she was almost as surprised as her friend was.

The typewritten note and the rose were actually from Pastor Andrew?

He had been at the barn raising when Katie had received the letter and gift, but Carolina couldn't remember if he'd stayed to eat lunch. Had he seen her run out of the room crying?

No wonder the poor man was a bundle of nerves.

Carolina pushed Katie forward and tried to fade into the background so the couple could talk, but she didn't get far enough away that she couldn't hear what was going on between the two of them. This was just too good to miss.

And *so* romantic.

Her heart welled. She tried not to shift her gaze to Wyatt but failed miserably. She caught his eyes momentarily, gulped in a breath of air and forced herself to look away.

"That was *you*?" Katie finally found her voice.

Pastor Andrew's brow creased in confusion. "Of course it was me. I signed the note, didn't I?"

"It was typewritten."

"Yes. Well. Is—is that a problem?"

"No. It's just that I thought it must have been the mystery matchmakers at work. It wasn't handwritten, and a couple of boys delivered it."

Now it was Pastor Andrew's turn to redden. "That's the last time I try to be romantic," he mumbled under his breath.

Then, louder, he said, "I am so sorry. I can see now how you might have gotten the wrong impression. I typed the note because my handwriting is atrocious and I was afraid you wouldn't be able to read it. Worse than a doctor's script, I can promise you. I can't even read my own writing sometimes. I wanted to let you know I was interested, but instead I made you believe the exact opposite.

"I had the boys deliver the letter because—oh, never mind what I was thinking about. What matters is what you think, Katie."

"What I think?" Katie parroted, her voice still high and squeaky.

"About what I said in the note. You know—the question I asked?"

Pastor Andrew held his hand out to Katie and grinned. "Will you be my valentine?"

Carolina was happy for her friends. She really was. But she couldn't help the way her heart dipped as she considered her own circumstances.

There would be no valentine for her.

Chapter Seven

The nursing home orderlies showed up about an hour after the event started and relieved Wyatt of having to watch Gran.

No—*having* wasn't the right word. He was happy to spend time with Gran, to be her date, especially since she seemed to know who he was tonight. Granted, she'd gotten the part about his being married to Carolina wrong, but who could blame her? Past and present melded in her mind.

It was gratifying to see the joy in her eyes as she watched couples dance, and as she indulged in her own bit of perfection in the form of a bowl of chocolate ice cream smothered in hot fudge sauce. Chocolate on chocolate. The smile on her face when she looked at him was worth every bit of effort it had taken him to get her here.

But she tired easily and was more than ready when the orderlies appeared to take her away.

But now that Gran had been taken back to the nursing home, Wyatt wasn't sure what to do with himself. He probably would have left when Gran did, except Johnny had joined him and was in the midst of a major teenage meltdown.

Wyatt did not miss being that age, when every little thing felt like the end of the world.

Did the girl he admired like him? Did he dare ask her to dance?

At least Johnny's crisis helped Wyatt not chew his cud over his grandmother's mistaken impression that Carolina was his wife.

Why couldn't he let that thought go?

Johnny fidgeted beside him, clenching and unclenching his fists in an uneasy rhythm and muttering to himself under his breath.

"You're going to have to relax, pal." Wyatt laid a hand on the boy's shoulder. "You're hyperventilating. Your girl will probably notice you if you pass out, but I think it would be better for both of you if you didn't."

Johnny didn't laugh at Wyatt's pathetic attempt at humor. From time to time, the young man would glance across the room to where a small group of teenage girls huddled, but his gaze never lingered very long.

Wyatt conspiratorially bent his head toward Johnny. "So which one is she, again?"

Johnny had spoken of Cassie Kramer, a pretty

girl he knew from the high school he attended. Johnny hadn't said much, but Wyatt had poked around a little bit and discovered Cassie was in the homecoming court and a star player on the girls' basketball team. She hadn't let her popularity go to her head, as Wyatt remembered the girls often doing when he was in high school. Rather, Johnny said she always smiled at him and sometimes stopped to talk in the hall, never belittling him for his stutter.

"The b-brunette," Johnny answered, shifting from one foot to another. "The p-pretty one."

Wyatt had no idea what constituted beauty in a modern teenager, so he took a guess. "The one in the pink sweater? You're right. She is pretty."

Johnny nodded so voraciously that a large lock of his curly dark hair dropped over his forehead.

"S-so is C-Carolina. She's w-wearing red."

Wyatt's eyebrows shot up and then he narrowed his eyes on his teenage protégé, He hadn't mentioned anything to Johnny about the note he had received, especially the part about Carolina wearing red.

Which meant…

He'd found his mystery matchmaker.

But why would Johnny want to set him up with Carolina? He decided to play along.

Wyatt smiled slyly and winked at Johnny. "Yeah. I noticed."

He tried not to hazard a glance at Carolina but couldn't seem to help himself. She was standing alone in the corner, her arms crossed in front of her as if she were cold, even though it was quite warm in the building. Wyatt felt a trickle of sweat run down his spine.

He turned his attention back to Johnny.

"So. This Cassie girl. Are you going to ask her to dance, or what?"

The stain on Johnny's cheeks intensified. Johnny gaped at him and shook his head.

"I could n-never—"

"Why not?" Wyatt wasn't much of a judge about such things, but despite the young man's shyness and stutter, he was a nice enough kid in both looks and personality. And he was as loyal as they came. A girl could do worse.

"C-Cassie is—" Johnny didn't finish his sentence.

"Cassie is standing right over there waiting for you to go and ask her to dance. She's glanced your way several times now."

His eyes widened. "At m-me?"

"Yes, at you. Don't sound so surprised." Wyatt nodded toward Cassie. "Go."

Johnny had always taken Wyatt's advice, so he was taken aback when the teenager shook his head.

"You aren't d-dancing. Neither is C-Carolina."

"I don't dance."

Johnny shrugged. "N-neither do I."

Wyatt could see where this was going. Johnny was continuing to play matchmaker, although after Gran's surprise statement this evening it seemed the boy would have to get in line for that particular job. Still, Wyatt was surprised at Johnny's sudden gumption. Who knew that the teenager had a stubborn streak?

"I see. So let me get this straight. The deal is that if I dance with Carolina, you will dance with Cassie?"

Johnny hesitated, then nodded.

"Okay."

"Okay?" Wyatt hadn't really expected Johnny to go for it. Now he was in a fix, but he could hardly back out now that he'd stuck his foot in his mouth. He ran a hand across his jaw. "All right, then. Let's do it."

He shook Johnny's hand to seal the deal and watched as the teen crossed the room toward his crush.

Smooth move, Harrow.

Now what was he going to do? What was Carolina going to think when he approached her with this crazy scheme? But there was no point lingering. He had to ask, even if she laughed him out of the building.

He took a deep breath and headed toward Carolina, reminding himself that this was no more difficult than what he'd just asked Johnny to do. When he reached Carolina's side, he held out his hand to her.

"Help a guy out here, huh?"

He meant Johnny, of course, and he glanced over his shoulder to see how the boy was doing. Johnny was standing right next to Cassie, his hands shyly jammed into the front pockets of his oversized jeans. He and Cassie weren't yet headed for the dance floor, but at least she'd apparently welcomed him into the conversation with her friends.

Could be worse.

Like standing here with his arm extended when there was zero response from the woman he'd just asked to dance.

Not a positive response, at any rate. Carolina was staring at his hand as if he were holding a big, hairy spider on his palm.

She gradually met his gaze and raised an eyebrow.

"What?" he muttered.

"I think that should be my question."

"It's a simple yes or no."

"To?"

He huffed out a breath. She knew how difficult this was for him and she was going to make him ask her twice. She was enjoying this *way* too much, if the amused gleam in her eye was anything to go by.

"Dance. Do you want to dance with me, or not?"

"Dance? You want to dance? With *me*?" Her expression was so full of astonishment he would almost think she hadn't known that was what he had been asking her all along.

"Yes, with you. What else did you think I would be asking you?"

"I can't imagine. But you don't dance."

"No. I don't. But I'm making an exception just this once, for a good cause."

The lights in the fellowship hall had been turned off, replaced by the glow of several party lamps that sent soft, swirling balls of muted color—green, blue and red—swirling around the room. It was difficult for Wyatt to tell for certain, but he was fairly positive her color heightened when she placed her hand in his.

It felt right, though, somehow, when he closed his hand over hers and led her out to the dance floor, and even more when he turned and took her into his arms. Their eyes met and locked and his breath hitched in his throat.

All of a sudden, he forgot all about Johnny and the initial reason he had asked her to dance. The people around them faded away and his pulse echoed to the slow, steady beat of the music.

Her hand slid from his shoulder to his chest until her palm covered his heart. The warmth in her eyes spread through him like honey.

His gaze dropped to her full lips, which were tinted with a sparkling red gloss that perfectly matched her blouse.

She was wearing red.

Well, of course she was. Half the women in the room were wearing red. It was Valentine's Day, after all, so it wasn't a huge stretch that she'd decided to wear that color.

But was it possible she'd received a note from the mystery matchmakers similar to the one that had shown up at his door?

Was she sending him a message?

"You're wearing red," he murmured, bending his head so he could whisper into her ear. His lips were close enough that he thought she might be able to feel him smile.

She pushed against him.

Hard.

What?

Confusion spun through him.

He leaned back enough to put space between them, but he didn't release her from his arms.

"People are watching us," she hissed in a low, scratchy voice.

He'd been so caught up in the moment that he'd

completely forgotten there *were* people around them who could be watching.

He blinked, his head still fuzzy.

She was right. Whatever had been about to happen between them shouldn't be happening. This wasn't the best idea he'd ever had, particularly not in public.

But then again, he really hadn't been thinking at all.

He furtively glanced around them and was relieved to find no one was paying particular attention to them—no one except Johnny, who still stood in the midst of the group of girls. The teenager was staring right at them and grinning like a blooming madman.

Wyatt couldn't fathom why, but his being with Carolina seemed particularly important to Johnny.

Wait a minute. He was only out here on the dance floor with Carolina in the first place for Johnny's sake—or at least, that was his excuse, and he was going to stick with it.

Johnny, on the other hand, wasn't keeping his end of the bargain.

Wyatt mock frowned and nodded his head toward Cassie. Johnny looked down, clearly gathering his courage, and then tapped Cassie on the shoulder and gestured toward the dance floor.

There was a long moment when Cassie hesitated and Wyatt held his breath. If she blew Johnny off, then Wyatt would be responsible for getting his hopes up, only to see them dashed upon the ragged rocks of reality, as had happened to Wyatt. The last thing Johnny needed was another reason for him to doubt himself.

Cassie said something to the group of girls and then put her arm around Johnny's waist and smiled up at him.

Wyatt let out the breath he'd been holding in an audible whoosh of air. Relief flooded through him.

Carolina followed the direction of his gaze.

"It looks like Johnny's having fun. Is that his girlfriend?"

"Not yet." He smiled down at her. "But he'd like her to be."

"It looks like he's getting a good start, then. They are a cute couple."

"Yeah. They are. I think Johnny is still really nervous though. He's stumbling over his feet. I hope he can relax enough to enjoy his dance."

"Why aren't you?"

"Enjoying the dance?"

Oh, but he was. Too much, in fact.

"Stumbling over your feet. I thought you said you don't dance."

"I said I *don't* dance. Not that I *can't* dance.

Gran made me take lessons when I was a kid. Ballroom dancing." He cringed at the memory.

"Well, the lessons paid off. You should give your gran an extra hug next time you see her."

The gap between them lessened as a new song started and their eyes once again met and held.

"You mentioned the fact that I am wearing red," she said thoughtfully.

He shrugged, not wanting to get into the whole mystery matchmaker thing if he had been the only one to receive a letter from them.

"Yeah, well, I guess that's no big surprise, is it, seeing as it's Valentine's Day and all. R-red is a good color on you, by the way."

Oh, brother. He was starting to stutter as badly as Johnny. And he was feeling just a little bit weak in the knees.

"Thank you." She smiled sweetly, then paused and pursed her lips. "But I have to be honest. The red blouse wasn't entirely my idea."

He immediately froze on the spot, a chill skittering down his spine.

She shook her head. "I got a letter—ostensibly signed by you—suggesting I should meet you here at the ice cream social wearing red, as a beacon or something."

"It wasn't from me," he felt obligated to point out, although his heart warmed with hope.

Despite, or because of, the letter, she had worn

red. Was she trying to tell him there might be a chance for them? That maybe—it would take a lot of work and forgiveness on both of their parts—but maybe they could eventually be a real family together?

Wyatt, Carolina and Matty?

That notion didn't seem quite as far off as it once had been.

"No. I know it wasn't from you," she hastened to add. "Katie told me all about the mystery matchmakers and how they are trying to set up couples all over town."

"They're fairly accurate, too."

She chuckled. "So I hear. Anyway, I would have figured it out myself even without Katie's explanation. The note was presumably signed by you, but the script was too juvenile. Even after all these years, I would recognize your handwriting if I saw it. Besides, I knew you wouldn't be asking me to a Valentine's *anything*."

Well, she was right about that. He wouldn't have asked her out.

Would he?

Holding her close in his arms now, swaying gently to the music, he wasn't so sure.

"And yet you wore red. Weren't you afraid you'd be encouraging the little rascals? Or worse yet, me?" He grinned like a hyena.

"It is the only blouse I own that fits the theme."

"Lady in Red." He nodded in appreciation, his chest filling with emotion.

"Anyway, my outfit won't set nearly as many tongues wagging as people seeing you and me out on the dance floor together."

"True."

"And yet, here we are."

He arched his eyebrows and grinned even wider. "Yes, we are."

"I'm glad."

The warmth in her eyes was too much for him. He looked away.

Johnny and Cassie were dancing nearby, and the boy was beaming with delight. Wyatt didn't envy Johnny his teenage awkwardness and angst, but he remembered what dancing with his first crush felt like.

That memory didn't hold a candle to dancing with his first and only true love.

"Yeah. I'm glad, too," he said through a dry throat. "Just look at them. They can't get enough of each other."

Carolina stopped dancing. "Them?"

She turned, following his gaze.

"Johnny?" Her voice sounded stilted, somehow, as if her feelings were hurt. "Oh. I get it."

She whirled on him but didn't step back into his embrace. He felt the emptiness both in his arms and in his heart.

"You are doing this because of Johnny." Her tone and her eyes dared him to deny it.

For a moment, he considered doing just that. He was confused. Why should that matter?

But if he told her anything less than the whole truth, she would know he was lying. He'd never been good at hiding anything from her.

"Well, yes. I told Johnny I would ask you to dance if he would ask Cassie but—"

"Right. I—I should have known. I—" She paused and pressed her palms down her long, flowing black skirt. "If you'll excuse me, I need to go check on Matty."

He didn't know what to say. He wasn't sure he could have said anything if he'd tried. All he could do was watch her walk away from him, knowing he wouldn't be seeing her again any time soon.

Why couldn't he learn when to shut up? For once, things had been going well between them, and he had opened his mouth and blown it. Now, who knew what it would take for him to get back in Carolina's good graces?

He didn't have a clue how to fix this, but somehow it had to be done. His relationship with Matty depended on it.

But if he was being honest, it was more than that.

Much more.

* * *

Carolina seriously considered not going to work on Monday, but thankfully Wyatt never came around the office. She didn't know whether it was because of what had happened between them at the Valentine's social or whether he just had a heavy docket of ranch calls, but either way, she was grateful for the temporary reprieve.

But when he didn't show up on Tuesday morning, she started to wonder. And worry. She might not quite be ready to face him yet, but she was just going to have to get over herself and prepare for the eventuality of being around Wyatt without it sending her into a dither every single time.

Wyatt was now a part of Matty's life. The mature, responsible thing for Carolina to do would be to seek Wyatt out and speak to him about what had happened between them at the Valentine's social, adult to adult, and clear the air about it so they could move on.

Right this second she was really tired of *adulting*.

She wanted to go hide in her room like a brokenhearted teenager.

Brokenhearted?

Where had that come from? That was impossible. She would have to be in love with Wyatt in order for him to break her heart, and she'd left that emotion behind long ago. She wasn't even certain she had a heart to break anymore.

So maybe not a broken heart, then. But she was certainly feeling something almost as uncomfortable. Not being able to define her feelings was not helping matters any.

Despite her best efforts, she'd grown to care about Wyatt. How could she not? They were forever connected through Matty. Watching Wyatt parent their child gave a new meaning to the word *love*, one that she could accept and embrace. There was nothing in the world like the bonding that occurred between a man and his son.

Carolina fumbled for the phone on her desk and picked up the receiver, punching in Wyatt's cell phone number before she could talk herself out of it again.

He picked up on the first ring.

"We need to talk," she said without preamble.

Silence met her on the other end of the line.

"Wyatt?"

Had he hung up on her?

"Yeah. Okay. You're right." She heard him draw in a ragged breath. "I'm heading your direction. The farrier is meeting me at my stable to trim some of the horses' hooves, and one threw a shoe the other day. If I leave now, we should have a few minutes to talk before he gets there."

"I'll keep an eye out for your truck and meet you at the stable."

"You'll have Matty with you?"

"Yes. Of course."

"Great. I thought he might like to watch Nick work on the horses."

"I'm sure he will be fascinated by it. I'll see you in a few minutes."

She hung up the phone and sighed deeply.

There. That wasn't so bad.

"Come on, Matty," she said, scooping him out of the play yard she had set up for him. "Let's go see your—"

Daddy.

Her gut tightened.

It was time.

And it was the right thing to do.

If they told Matty the truth now, the toddler would most likely never remember there had been a time when Wyatt wasn't a part of his life— though however large or small a part that ended up being was still up in the air.

Instead of waiting in the office for Wyatt to arrive at the ranch, Carolina took Matty to the stable and let him pet some of the horses, moving down the lane stall by stall. She inhaled the reassuring pungency of hay, horses and something else, an unidentifiable scent that was somehow unique to Wyatt's stable. It was probably the country girl in her, but for some reason the blend of scents soothed her.

It felt like home.

The names of each of Wyatt's horses were engraved on a wooden plaque on every stall door, and Carolina introduced her son to each horse by name.

Bash the Appaloosa, Cricket the palomino, and a beautiful paint named Chief.

When they reached the end of the row, Carolina grabbed a couple of apples from a nearby bushel and they started back the way they'd come. The stalls on the opposite side were filled with various animals Wyatt was vetting and keeping for observation. In one stall they found a sow and some cute little piglets. In another, a curious llama. And in a third, a couple of bleating goats.

"Goats!" Matty announced.

"That's right, buddy."

They paused by a pretty black mare and Matty giggled in delight as Carolina showed him how to feed the horse an apple. Even Carolina chuckled as the mare crunched on the sweet fruit, smacking her lips and showing her teeth as juice ran down her muzzle. When the mare was done, she nudged Matty's outstretched hand, looking for another treat.

"I see you found Juliet," Wyatt said as he entered the barn. "She is one of the boys ranch horses. She pulled a ligament in her leg, so I've been keeping her here for a couple of weeks to monitor her progress and do some physical therapy with her."

Carolina's eyes met Wyatt's, and a long, awkward pause followed as Carolina struggled to find the right words to express the emotions she was feeling.

Wyatt held out his arms to Matty and the toddler launched himself at his daddy, his high, youthful laugh blending with Wyatt's deeper one.

Wyatt opened the stall door and stepped inside, plunking their son onto the back of the horse.

"There you go, cowboy."

A surge of anxiety flooded through Carolina. The black was a large draft horse, and a fall would be disastrous.

"Is that safe?"

Wyatt's gaze widened on her as if she'd just said something completely outrageous—which, she guessed in hindsight, she had. She was no stranger to country living. Most of the folks who'd grown up in Haven had been riding almost as long as they'd been walking. And the draft appeared gentle.

Besides, it wasn't as if Wyatt had placed Matty on the tall mount and then walked away. Wyatt's hand was still spanning Matty's waist and the toddler had his fist tightly threaded through the mare's thick mane.

"Sorry," she apologized. "I'm being a helicopter mom again. It's a bad habit of mine."

"I don't even know what that means."

"It's like we were talking about in the park. I have the tendency to hover over Matty, worry too much about him getting hurt trying new things. I guess it's just a residual response from when I was raising him all on my own—trying to be both a mother and a father to him."

Wyatt made a low, indistinguishable sound from deep in his throat, part groan, part growl.

She held up her hands to stop him before he stated the obvious.

"I know. I know. That was entirely my own fault, born of the poor decisions I personally chose to make. I hope someday you'll find it in your heart to forgive me."

She took a deep breath and let it out slowly. Her spirit felt lightened, unburdened, now that she'd finally admitted her mistakes out loud, and to Wyatt.

His gaze narrowed and he pressed his lips into a thin, hard line. Carolina could see he was trying to suppress his urge to share his own opinions on her *choices*.

She took a deep breath and bolted ahead with her thoughts before she lost her nerve.

"That was one of the things I need to talk to you about today."

She gathered her thoughts as she considered how to approach the subject, about how it was time for Matty to know Wyatt was his daddy and how they were going to work out the logistics of sharing him between them. What they had now, with Carolina employed in Wyatt's office, was working out wonderfully. But what would happen once Wyatt took off to do service on foreign soil? What would that mean for Matty?

For her?

She coughed to remove the strangling sensation in her throat. "For starters, though, I think we need to address what happened on the dance floor the other night."

His gaze didn't waver, but his shoulders visibly tightened and a tic of strain showed at the taut corner of his whiskered jaw.

"Nothing happened." His voice was scraping as coarse as sandpaper.

"Almost happened, then," she modified.

"What are you getting at, Carolina? We don't have much more time left before Nick gets here. If you have something that you want to say to me, just spit it out."

The harshness of his tone caused her emotions to scuttle, crab-like, back into the shell of her heart.

So much for being vulnerable. Clearly she'd misread all the signals—or maybe there hadn't been any to begin with. Was her imagination running overtime? Or maybe there were unresolved emotions lingering.

"What do you want Matty to call you?" She barely got the words out. But if he wanted a change of topic, he'd just been belted with the best one she had.

"I—" He paused to lift his hat and brush a palm back through his hair. "What do you mean?"

"I think it's time to be truthful with Matty. It's not fair to him or to you to go on the way we're doing. I know that you have plans for the future, and I don't want what has happened between us to change those intentions, but I also know you want to be part of Matty's life." She gulped for air but found none. "So what I want to know is this. Have you thought about what you'd like Matty to call you? He refers to me as Mama."

Carolina had only once in her life seen Wyatt cry. That was the night he'd been certain he was about to lose his gran. The night Matty was conceived. But now Wyatt's beautiful dark eyes turned glassy and he took a deep breath to steady himself, grasping for the stall door.

"You mean, like *Daddy*?"

His voice was shaking with emotion, and Carolina couldn't help but smile at him.

"Yes. That's exactly what I mean."

"Daddy," Wyatt breathed.

"Daddy!" Matty echoed excitedly.

Somehow the toddler had managed to tuck his legs underneath him on the horse's back, and he sprang at Wyatt without forewarning.

Carolina was grateful for Wyatt's quick reflexes. He gave an audible *oomph* as Matty slammed into his chest, but Wyatt held the boy tight and kissed the top of his head.

"What did you say, little guy?"

"Daddy." Matty beamed with pride.

Carolina marveled at the fact that their son appeared to have had no trouble at all following their conversation, nor segueing from *Mr. Wyatt* to *Daddy*. And here she'd been worried about how they could possibly explain the concept of fatherhood to a toddler.

She'd been reluctant partially because she was worried about how Matty would handle the transition, but she saw now that she shouldn't have been. Children had the amazing capacity to embrace love and to keep things simple that adults always managed to complicate. It was the other part of the equation—when the man Matty would come to depend on went away—that worried her. She and Wyatt would have to deal with that issue when the time came, but right now, it was enough that Wyatt was acknowledging his relationship with his son.

"Daddy it is, then," Wyatt choked out emotionally.

Carolina wandered down the line of stalls, intending to give Wyatt and Matty a moment of personal space for them both to adapt to this new, happy reality. She passed another llama and then paused by the stall that held the yearling buck they had rescued.

She'd asked after it a few times and Wyatt had indicated that all was going well with the deer. In fact, he had said he was planning to release the young buck back into the wild sometime during the coming week.

She'd expected to see a healthy deer, possibly suspicious of her presence and definitely eager to get out of the tiny stall and back into the grassy world in which he belonged.

Instead, the buck was lying on its side, much like when she'd first seen it, although this time it was cushioned by a light covering of hay on the floor of the stall.

She obviously wasn't an expert on animals, but there was something *off* in the way the deer was lying. Its legs were sticking straight out to the side instead of folded up underneath it, and the gash on its haunches was smeared with fresh wet blood.

"Wyatt," she called.

"What is it?" He walked toward her with Matty in his arms, the joyful light in his eyes echoed by his beaming smile.

"Is the buck still supposed to be bleeding?"

The grin dropped from Wyatt's lips as he strode forward and thrust Matty into Carolina's waiting arms. He slipped into the stall and knelt before the deer, running a comforting hand down the buck's quivering neck.

"What happened?" He sounded genuinely perplexed and, more than that, dejected.

In short order, Wyatt had wet a towel and washed out the wound. It was one of the original gashes from when the deer had been hit by the truck, but for some reason, instead of healing, there were now angry red flames of infection around the laceration.

"I don't understand. He was getting better." Carolina couldn't miss the note of discouragement in his tone.

"Could he have hit himself on something in the stall and reopened the wound?"

"I don't know. Maybe." Wyatt's voice scraped out a frustrated growl. "But I don't see how. There's nothing in the stall sharp enough to do any real damage. This gash is seriously infected. I've managed up until now to keep all of the wounds clean and covered, and now this happens."

"But he'll get better, right? Will you be able to—" her throat closed and she had difficulty finishing her sentence "—save the poor thing?"

Wyatt shook his head. "I don't know. It's bad. I may have to put it down, after all."

Seething with frustration, he planted his fist into his open palm and grumbled something unintelligible.

Carolina's heart hurt for him. Wyatt genuinely cared. That was what made him such a good veterinarian.

But this? This felt like it was more than just the typical situation with an animal Wyatt vetted, as if he had formed a special bond with the creature.

Wyatt thoroughly cleaned the wound with antiseptic and wrapped it with layers of gauze. Carolina guessed the fuzzy-antlered buck would probably make short work of the dressing, but she hoped he would ignore it so the wound would stay clean and covered.

Nick McGarrett, who often did farrier work for Wyatt, entered just as Wyatt was finishing up. Wyatt was clearly still distracted by the ailing buck, but he turned his attention to the horses.

"I thought I would spend a little time this afternoon putting together some plans for Gran's birthday party," Carolina said. "It looks like you two are going to be busy." She eyed the farrier's tools, some of which didn't look particularly safe for a curious two-year-old boy to be near. "Would you like me to take Matty back to the office with me? I'd hate for him to get underfoot and be a bother to you."

Wyatt took Matty's hand and smiled down at him. The boy beamed back at his daddy. "He won't be a bother. He's my big boy, right, Matty?"

She started to tell Wyatt to be careful but bit the inside of her lip to keep the words from tumbling out of her mouth.

There was absolutely no question that Wyatt was going to take care of Matty. He'd probably be even more attentive than she would have been.

No more helicopter mom for her. She had to let go of all her fears and worries for their son. Wyatt could handle Matty just fine for a while on his own, and they needed time to bond. There wasn't anyone else on the planet, after Carolina, who cared as much about Matty as Wyatt did. After all, he was the boy's *daddy*.

Chapter Eight

Trimming the horses' hooves was a routine procedure that every ranch had done on a regular basis, and yet Wyatt was breathing in the experience as if for the first time, seeing everything through Matty's curious eyes. As Nick worked, Wyatt explained what the farrier was doing—how he got the horse to trust him enough to lift its legs, and what he was doing with the files, hammers and nippers.

Nick even let Matty place his little hands over Nick's larger ones, allowing the toddler to "help" him file. Everything was going well at first, but then Matty got a little overexcited and his happy squeal and flapping arms set the already anxious gelding skittering to the side.

"Whoa, there," Wyatt said, pushing against the horse's flank and scooping Matty safely out of the way.

Wyatt frowned. He needed to pay closer attention to what was happening with his son. Maybe a stall with a nervous horse and a busy farrier wasn't the safest place for a toddler to be, after all.

It was bad enough that Wyatt couldn't seem to keep his mind from wandering back to where things had gone wrong with the injured buck. He couldn't toss off the idea that he could have done more to save the deer, even if rationally he knew otherwise.

But he knew his feelings came from the heart, which was what made the whole thing so devastating. He'd somehow become invested in this buck—and far more than that, so had Carolina and Matty.

He didn't want to disappoint them. They would both be brokenhearted if he had to put the buck down.

Wyatt sighed and brushed the dark hair off Matty's forehead. He had passed strike three in making mistakes as a new father a long time ago. This felt more like he was striking right out of the game, maybe even the season.

Swing, miss. Swing, miss.

He probably should have taken Carolina up on her offer to watch Matty, but he so desperately wanted to spend every waking moment with his son, to teach him all the things a boy should learn from his father.

His heart did a somersault every time he heard Matty's sweet, innocent voice calling him Daddy.

But maybe he was trying to do too much too fast. Wyatt could and would teach the boy how to care for the ranch animals, but clearly he was overcompensating for the time he had missed, and he had to remind himself that Matty was only two years old. He wouldn't be shoeing horses for a few years yet.

He had time, as long as Carolina didn't up and disappear out of his life again. Years' worth of time. Any thoughts of leaving Haven, of being separated from Matty for even one day, were long since behind him. He was Matty's father. He wouldn't disappear from the boy's life, no matter what that meant to his own prior vision of his future.

He had a new dream now, one that included his son—and even the boy's beautiful mother.

With effort, Wyatt turned back to his work. Nick had taken the mare out of the next stall and had haltered her loosely against a pole so he could replace the shoe she'd thrown.

Mercury, as her name suggested, was a bit of a bugger at times and she liked to bite—especially when people fiddled with her legs. Nick had been Wyatt's farrier for some time now and was well familiar with Mercury's bad habits, but there was only so much a man could do when a horse had sensitive legs and had been known to kick as well as use her teeth. The shoe still had to be fitted.

"Let me hold her head for you," Wyatt offered, knowing his presence would calm the mare down so the farrier could do his work with more ease.

Matty started wiggling, pumping his chunky arms and legs and pushing against Wyatt's chest so it was hard to hold the toddler in one arm.

"Down. Down," Matty insisted.

Now wasn't a good time to put the boy on the ground, but when Wyatt tried to calm him, he became even more adamant, making the calm horses in the other stalls skittish, and that was nothing to say of further agitating Mercury.

Wyatt looked around for a solution.

Just inside the barn door, framed in a ray of sunshine, was Blitzy, one of Wyatt's young goats.

Wyatt breathed a sigh of relief and dropped Matty down by Blitzy, who was just the right size for a toddler to play with, without fear that the goat would knock him over or create too much havoc. Fortunately, this particular goat was among the friendliest Wyatt owned, and he was sure the animal would be up to a little friendly petting.

Besides, Wyatt would only be a few steps away. He stepped back to the mare's head and smoothed a hand down her neck as Nick took his position at the mare's left hind leg.

"Easy, there, girl," Wyatt soothed.

Mercury snorted her disdain and tried to toss her head when the farrier picked up her foot, but Wyatt held tight and didn't let her move. She shifted and struck out with her back legs in a half buck, but Nick was an old hand at his work and managed to avoid getting a hoof in the face.

Nick chuckled. "Stubborn old goat, isn't she?"

At the word *goat*, Wyatt's gaze slid over to Matty, expecting the boy and his new four-legged friend to be playing together, safe, sound and secure.

Instead, he discovered that Matty had somehow led the goat to the side of the barn, where a partially used bale of hay had been tossed up against the wall.

It took Wyatt just two seconds too long to figure out what Matty was trying to do.

Wyatt slipped underneath the mare's neck and darted toward Matty, just as the toddler scooted on top of the hay bale and scrambled onto the goat's back.

Wyatt and Matty's voices were simultaneous, one terrified, the other exultant.

"Matty, no!"

"Go, goat!"

At the sudden extra load wiggling on its back,

the goat reared and bolted, catching Matty un-
aware. The toddler flipped forward off the goat's
back and somersaulted twice before hitting the
edge of the barn door.

Wyatt dived toward him but missed getting his
hands under the boy by inches.

Matty sent up a spine-chilling wail.

This wasn't just the sound of a scared little
boy. This was a pain cry. And Wyatt knew with
gut-wrenching certainty that Matty was seriously
injured.

"Oh, Lord, please. Not Matty," he breathed.

God had to be there. He just *had* to listen. Not
because of Wyatt, who didn't deserve a moment's
notice from the Almighty, but for Matty. The kid
was an innocent. He didn't deserve to be hurt because of Wyatt's negligence.

He felt like throwing up as he scooped his son
into his arms as gently as he could and tried to
soothe him with whispered words. Matty had
been injured on *his* watch.

Carolina would never forgive him.

He would never forgive himself.

But despite his own sense of humiliation and
disgrace over what had just happened, he didn't
pause at all before running straight for the office.

For Carolina.

She was going to be so, so angry.

But she was a nurse, and Matty's mom. She would know what to do, how to help him.

Wyatt was beyond thinking rationally. His son was hurt—his beloved son. And it was all his fault. Guilt and shame poured over him like thick, wet cement.

"What happened?" Carolina asked as Wyatt kicked the already partially open door wide with the toe of his boot.

"I goofed up," Wyatt admitted bluntly. "I goofed up, and now Matty is injured."

Carolina appeared not to have heard his words. Her eyes—and her full attention—were on Matty.

"Where does it hurt, baby?"

Matty tried to lift up his right arm and then wailed in pain, clutching his hand to his chest. "Owie!"

Wyatt cringed at the sound, and even more when he saw the little boy's face crumple. It was like a punch in his already churning gut. He wanted to try to explain what had happened and why he had let Matty down, but he knew Carolina wasn't interested in his excuses.

Not now. Maybe not ever.

Carolina took Matty's right arm and examined it from his fingertips to his shoulder.

"I think he may have fractured his wrist. It might just be a few torn ligaments, but he's having difficulty moving it. At the very least he has hyperextended his thumb. We'll have to get his hand x-rayed to know for certain." She picked up a stray board. "I'm going to stabilize his hand until we can get him to the doctor. I'll need a roll of gauze."

She sounded amazingly calm and collected, considering what she was saying, and she expertly wrapped Matty's arm within minutes.

"We need to get in to see Dr. Delgado right away." She flashed him a measured look, sizing him up. "Do you think you can drive?"

That might very well have been an insult, but she was right to ask. Wyatt still wasn't thinking clearly, and he was shaking like a leaf in a thunderstorm.

He inhaled deeply through his nose and set his jaw. He'd let Matty down once. He *would* be there for his son.

"Let's go."

"Use my sedan. Matty's car seat is already attached in the backseat and it will take us less time."

Wyatt made a mental note to buy a car seat for Matty to use in his dual-cab truck.

Carolina reached for Matty, making soothing noises as she tossed Wyatt her car keys. He slid behind the wheel while Carolina buckled Matty in the back. The boy's crying had mellowed out and he was quietly sniffling, but Carolina still rode in the back with him to reassure him and keep him from getting agitated again.

Glancing in the rearview mirror, Wyatt caught a rare glimpse of vulnerability on Carolina's face—an emotion she usually kept well hidden.

Shame filled him. He wished he could shift the blame for this particular episode onto someone or something else—the goat, or the skittish horse.

But no.

This was all on him.

They'd just today made the decision to have Matty address him as Daddy—

Just in time for him to prove definitively that he shouldn't be one at all.

Once they'd reached Dr. Delgado's office, it didn't take long for him to determine that Carolina was correct in her diagnosis of Matty's injury. Sure enough, Dr. Delgado x-rayed the toddler's wrist and found a hairline fracture. He also suspected a torn ligament or two.

Determining the need to set Matty's wrist in a soft cast, the doctor gave Matty a dose of liquid ibuprofen and left the room to gather the necessary supplies.

Matty, for the most part, already seemed to be over the trauma of his misadventure and hardly noticed his owie. Dr. Delgado had given him a toy helicopter to play with and Matty was zooming it around in the air with his uninjured hand, oblivious to the purple, swollen appendage Carolina was gently trying to keep as still and stable as possible on his lap.

Wyatt, on the other hand, looked absolutely terrible. His face was as white as a sheet and his gaze carried the glassy-eyed panic of a cornered animal. His Adam's apple was bobbing as if he were having difficulty swallowing, and more than once she saw him brush away a tear. Clearly, Matty's accident had really shaken him.

To Carolina, his tears weren't a sign of weakness, but of great strength, although she knew Wyatt wouldn't think so. He would be appalled if he thought she'd even noticed them, so she withheld the urge to reach out and take his hand to let him know that Matty would be fine, and that she didn't blame him for the injury.

Carolina remembered the first time Matty had ever had a serious accident. He'd just been learning to pull himself into a standing position, and yet the little fellow had somehow managed to leverage himself up and roll over the top edge of his playpen.

Hearing a sound, she had glanced over at him from the couch, where she had been watching television, and had recognized too late what was about to happen. From that point it had been like she was in slow motion. She'd rushed toward him when she'd realized he was going to fall, but she'd been too late to catch him. Thankfully, he hadn't landed directly on his head, and the floor was carpeted. He'd naturally tucked and rolled and his shoulder had taken the brunt of the impact. She'd watched him like a hawk for days afterward, hovering over him and looking for possible signs of concussion.

The blame she'd felt had been crippling.

She'd soon learned that mischievous little boys bumped their heads and scraped their knees on a regular basis—and yet they survived and thrived. This new tumble was just one more accident among many, past and future. She had learned not to obsess about every little thing or she would go crazy. Boys will be boys, and all that.

But for Wyatt, this was his first experience seeing his kid get hurt, and she could tell how hard he was taking it. He was gripping Matty's knee like a lifeline. His head was bowed and his lips were silently moving.

Praying?

But Wyatt had set his relationship with God aside long ago, when he was still a child and had suddenly and traumatically lost his parents.

Was it possible that something good would come from the bad, that these circumstances might drive Wyatt to his knees and remind him of his need of a Savior?

Carolina reached out her free hand and laid it over Wyatt's.

"Do you want to pray together?"

He jerked in response, and his astonished gaze burned into hers. She held her breath as the silence lingered.

"Pray?" he rasped, his voice sounding disconnected from the word. "That's what I—"

She nodded in understanding.

He paused and his eyes widened. "Yes. I'd like to pray with you. Pray for Matty. But it's been a long time and I—er, can you…?"

"Absolutely." Carolina nodded again and squeezed his hand tightly.

He bowed his head and closed his eyes, then turned his hand over and threaded his fingers through hers.

Her heartbeat quickened. Just look at the three of them. Wyatt, Carolina and the beautiful son with whom they'd been blessed. All circled together. They were a—

Family.

Her heart leaped into her throat and she wasn't sure she'd be able to speak out loud.

But Matty needed to hear Carolina's faith in God being lived out by example, and Wyatt needed to *see* it—see the strength her beliefs offered her.

"Dear Lord," she began softly, "watch after

Your precious child Matty. Guide Dr. Delgado's hand as he sets the cast. And we humbly ask that Matty's wrist might come out of this even stronger than it was before."

Wyatt's hand was quivering.

She paused to gather her thoughts. "We thank You, Jesus, for Your Holy Wounds, by which we ask this blessing today. In the name of the Father, and of the Son, and of the Holy Spirit. Amen."

Wyatt tried to echo her *amen* but all that came out of his mouth was a scratchy sound scraped from the depths of his throat.

He remained silent and thoughtful and continued to hold her hand while Carolina kept Matty distracted and occupied with his little plastic airplane. She suspected motor noises were more in Wyatt's skill set than hers, but she didn't want to push him when he was clearly in an introverted and reflective mood. She sent up a silent prayer that God was working on his heart and opening him up to faith.

When Dr. Delgado returned, his arms loaded with gauze, cotton and tape, Wyatt quickly jerked back, yanking his hand from hers and crossing his arms over his chest.

She didn't know why, but his action hurt her, bruised her already fragile self-esteem.

It shouldn't. But there it was.

Any thoughts Carolina might have had about

their being a family unit dissipated into thin air. Clearly Wyatt didn't want the doctor to get the wrong impression about them, that they might be a couple. Holding hands was off-limits, even if it had been for the very best of reasons.

They had been *praying* together. And there was nothing wrong with that.

When it came time to set the cast, Wyatt immediately stepped up to support Matty.

A muscle ticked in his taut jaw whenever the toddler made a distressed squeak, but his smile was encouraging and his words full of praise. He was a natural father, whether or not he thought he was.

"That's my big brave boy," Wyatt said as Dr. Delgado wrapped a cotton-like substance around his thumb and wrist that would keep it immobile and then packed it well up his forearm.

"Just like his daddy," Carolina agreed, automatically assisting the doctor with wetting the casting material and covering the cotton with it.

"We have to hold still for a few more minutes, honey," she said, knowing the cast needed time to set.

Dr. Delgado grinned. "I wish I had a place for you in my practice, Carolina. You would most certainly be an asset to me. Your nursing skills are outstanding."

"Thank you." She wished for that, as well—

or at least, she thought she did. Upon closer inspection she realized she had found a great deal of happiness working for Wyatt in his office, though of course she missed the direct interaction of helping people that nursing provided. With a little more administrative training, she thought she might actually find joy permanently working in Wyatt's office. But then, Wyatt hadn't offered her a permanent position. This was nothing more than a temporary solution to a difficult problem.

So much had changed since she'd returned to Haven. She realized she hadn't thought much about leaving. Instead, to her surprise, she was considering ways to stay.

When the cast had set, Dr. Delgado wrapped two stretch bandages over the whole area and then taped it up over the closures.

Matty was curious about his new cast and was trying out the weight of it, twisting his arm back and forth and laughing at how neat it was.

"He'll think it's really cool for about an hour, and then not so much," Dr. Delgado advised with a chuckle. "I'll need to see him back here in a week, although I suspect we may have to keep the cast on for a bit longer than that. The hard part is going to be trying to keep him out of trouble."

Carolina groaned. There was that.

Wyatt's face lost all its color.

"No goats," he muttered under his breath.

What was that about goats? Wyatt evidently had an interesting story to tell her. They'd been in such a rush to get to the doctor's office that they hadn't really had time to discuss *how* the accident had happened.

Dr. Delgado fitted Matty with a child-size sling covered with bright, primary-colored dinosaurs.

"Try to keep his arm in the sling as much as possible, but don't worry if he gets tired of wearing it sometimes. That hand is going to get heavy and the sling will help relieve the pressure on his shoulder muscles. Thankfully, he's not yet old enough for us to have to worry about it being his writing hand or him missing schoolwork."

"But he'll get better, right?" Wyatt asked, his voice lined with worry. "He won't have trouble using his hand?"

He'll get better.

It was the same question Carolina had asked about the deer, whose health had taken a major nosedive. But this wasn't the same thing at all.

"Yes, of course." Dr. Delgado smiled encouragingly. "Give him a few weeks and Matty here will be fully mended. He's so young right now that he won't even remember the time he broke his wrist."

Carolina eyed Wyatt as they walked back out to the parking lot with a sleepy Matty in Wyatt's arms. Clearly the excitement of the day was catching up with the toddler. Matty's head was tucked against Wyatt's shoulder and he was self-soothing by sucking on his fist.

Wyatt gently buckled the boy in his car seat. This time, Carolina chose to sit in the passenger seat opposite Wyatt so they could talk. Matty's eyes were already drooping and he would be sound asleep within minutes.

"You know, for a man who vets animals for a living, you looked a little green around the gills back there," she teased, trying to lighten the moment.

"Doctoring animals is *nothing* like seeing my own son in pain." He paused and inhaled a ragged breath. "Especially when it's all my fault that it happened."

Her first impulse was to tell him that he wasn't to blame, but belittling his feelings wasn't going to help him work through the incident and reconcile himself to what had happened. Not when he believed he was at fault for it.

She reached out and took his hand.

She thought he might pull away, but instead he tightened his grip on her fingers and sighed deeply.

"Do you want to talk about it?" she asked gently.

"It was a stupid goat. I can't believe I didn't see it coming. I looked away for one second and when I looked back, Blitzy was flinging Matty into the barn door."

"It attacked him?" Carolina was horrified, picturing a mean old billy goat butting her poor, defenseless little son. "Where did it come from?"

Wyatt shook his head. "No. It was nothing like that. As you know, I have a herd of young goats. Blitzy is small and super gentle, like the one I introduced Matty to a while ago. He seemed to really like goats, so I thought he would get a kick out of petting it while I held on to one of the horses' heads for Nick. You have to believe I thought Matty would be perfectly safe, or I never would have let him near the goat."

She waited for more of an explanation, but it didn't come. Wyatt remained silent, focused on the drive. She knew he had to work through the whole story or he would never forgive himself.

"But?" she prompted.

"But Matty was too fast for me. He got it into his head to *ride* the goat. I can't imagine what he was thinking."

"He's two, Wyatt. I doubt he considered the possible consequences."

Wyatt winced. "No. That was my responsibility."

She hadn't meant to point a finger at him, but rather to show him that he couldn't anticipate every eventuality. Not when it came to an active toddler.

"He crawled up on a hay bale and climbed aboard the startled animal. I figured out what Matty was about to do a split second before the whole thing unfolded before me like a bad dream—right about the time the *goat* figured out what he was about to do."

Carolina readjusted the picture in her mind to this new scene and couldn't help but chuckle.

Wyatt looked appalled. "You think this is funny?"

She tried to wipe the smile off her face, but it popped right back up again.

"No. Yes." Her fingers brushed across the pulse in her neck as she glanced back to check on Matty, who had fallen into a sound sleep, poor little guy.

"I'm not happy that Matty fractured his wrist, of course, but you'll have to admit the circumstances are amusing. This is one of those situations that aren't funny when they happen but will make hilarious stories around the family table years down the road."

"The family table, huh?" he repeated. She felt the tension go out of his grip, and he chuckled lightly. "Yeah. I guess you're right. But I lost ten years off my life when I saw Matty climb aboard that goat."

"You're a good dad, Wyatt," she assured him.

He scoffed. "I think I've just proven conclusively that I'm not."

"Because Matty had one little spill?"

"It was more than that and we both know it. He fractured his wrist. Frankly, Carolina, I don't think I am meant to be a dad."

She heartily disagreed.

"No one is *meant* to be a dad. You just are one. God blessed you with a son. You learn and adapt and make mistakes just like every other parent out there."

"But what if I make another bad judgment call and Matty gets hurt again?"

"I think it's more a matter of *when* than *if.* Not just for you, but for me, as well. We aren't infallible. Only God is. We can't see everything. We can't be there every single second of the day. We're going to blink. We're going to miss things. And when they fall…"

His eyes caught hers and his hold on her hand tightened.

"We pick them up again. We do what we can, but ultimately we have to give our son's welfare up to God. No one loves Matty more than He does. Not even us."

A smile slowly crept up one side of his lips. "I can't imagine a love that big. Someone who cares for Matty more than I do."

"Deeper and wider." Tears sprang to her eyes and she got all choked up when Wyatt voiced how very much he loved their son.

And to think she had once believed that it would be better that Wyatt never be a part of Matty's life.

Regret filled her. How very wrong she'd been. On so many levels.

They drove in silence the rest of the way back to Wyatt's ranch, each lost in their own thoughts. Matty was snoring lightly in the backseat. As a mother, she found his snorts and snores to be one of Matty's more endearing qualities—although his future wife might not be quite so keen on the trait. She smothered a laugh at the thought.

Wyatt pulled up in front of the house and cut the engine, which surprised Carolina because she figured she would just be dropping Wyatt off at his ranch and heading straight home to put Matty to bed. It had been an adventuresome and tiring day for all of them.

Maybe Wyatt still wanted to talk.

She had to admit she was curious.

He fisted his hands on the steering wheel and glanced in the rearview mirror.

"He's out like a light, isn't he?" Wyatt's voice was rich and deep and full of affection.

Carolina chuckled. "When he is sleeping soundly,

a tornado couldn't even wake him up. He gives a new meaning to *sleep like a baby*."

The corners of Wyatt's mouth rose but it wasn't his usually toothy grin, since his lips were pressed tightly together.

"I created email invitations for Gran's birthday party," she said to fill the silence. "I figured we could borrow the day room at the nursing home so she and her friends won't have to go too far out of their element."

"You were always very thoughtful."

Until she wasn't.

"Not always." Her mind darkened with the memory. This was a night for regrets.

He cleared his throat and turned toward her, his eyes a delicious dark chocolate. "I think we need to try to put the past behind us."

"For Matty's sake."

Her whole being, heart and soul, leaned in to him, hoping beyond hope that there was something more. That he would tell her that this wasn't just about Matty.

He nodded slowly, never breaking eye contact with her. "Yes. For Matty."

Her heart dropped like lead.

"But," he continued, as a tumble of emotion squeezed the air out of her lungs, "not *just* Matty."

He paused and reached for her, framing her face with one hand. His work-worn hands were scratchy against her cheek, but Carolina thought she'd never felt anything nicer. The chemistry ricocheting between them was infinitely familiar and yet paradoxically brand-new.

They weren't the same people they had been three years ago. They had both changed. Matured.

They had a son now.

"Carolina, I—"

He stopped abruptly.

She waited. She certainly couldn't say anything. Her capacity for speech had completely deserted her the moment Wyatt touched her.

"Back at the doctor's office? When we were praying together? That felt—well, it felt like we were a family. A *real* family. I want…I need to know if…"

He didn't finish his question, or statement, or whatever it was.

Instead, he brought his lips down on hers.

At first, his kiss was soft, a bare, butterfly-winged brush of his lips over hers. But then it turned urgent, hungry, as he pulled her closer and she wrapped her arms around his neck. He was seeking answers to the questions he could not voice, and yet he was communicating to her at the very same time.

A rush of warmth flooded her heart as she realized she was *home* in Wyatt's arms.

She never should have left.

Yet there was so much still unresolved between them.

They could no more have avoided this moment than they could have stopped the sun from shining. Strong emotions burned a path between them, as they always had, together with a deep longing to make what they had between them something better. Greater.

Forever.

The sum of two parts somehow incredibly equaling three. Maybe even more, in time.

But could he ever truly forgive her for taking Matty away from him? Could they work things out and move forward with their lives together? Even if she decided to make her permanent home in Haven, that didn't mean Wyatt would. What about all the ambitions he held? Years changed a person, but some dreams never altered. He'd been so sure that was what he wanted to do.

Could his dreams have changed?

Wyatt's lips, his gentle touch and the way he whispered her name between kisses—these all gave her reasons to hope, perhaps even to start believing in the possibility of a future between them.

And yet she knew that there was still a chasm between them that was so deep she was afraid to cross it.

She had no doubt that Wyatt believed he knew what he wanted *now*. But what about the future? *His* future?

Could he really give up his dreams in exchange for a staid and settled life with her and Matty? Could he stay here in Haven and truly be happy, without seeing all that was beyond the borders?

When push came to shove—would he *stay*?

Chapter Nine

Would she stay?

That had been the single most important question haunting Wyatt, a thread of doubt thrumming through his mind even at the exact moment that her soft, full lips had molded to his and a bouquet of warmth and emotion bloomed in his chest.

He'd gloried in the feel of her arms wrapped around his neck. He hadn't wanted to leave her embrace.

Not ever.

Especially when she'd burrowed her head on his chest, her ear resting next to his pounding heart. As he'd rested his chin against her hair and breathed in the scent of her, he had considered all the ways he wanted to care for her. Protect her.

Love her.

Those words frightened him. He'd been there

before, and the results had been catastrophic. He was still far too vulnerable, too gun-shy, to do anything but tread lightly. Their romantic relationship, assuming they ever had one, would take a long time to come to fruition, if it ever did.

She had run away from him once. He could not and would not risk his heart again—not until he knew for certain that she returned his love.

His heart wouldn't survive if she left again—especially because this time she had their son. He didn't want to fight for shared custody, but he couldn't be parted from his son. There was no way he would ever heal from that kind of pain.

So for now, his heart was officially on lockdown.

And he suspected she was feeling much the same way.

She hadn't said much after they'd kissed. She'd slid out of the passenger seat and walked around to the driver's side so she could take her sedan home. After he'd exited the vehicle, he'd grabbed her hand and tried to kiss her good-night, but she'd turned her head so his lips had brushed her cheek instead.

Already he could sense she was withdrawing from him. He didn't know why, but he was determined to stay the course this time—to show her all the reasons in the world why she ought to make Haven her permanent home.

And it wasn't just because of Matty.

He couldn't begin to read the woman's mind, but he was going to ask about her plans.

Flat out. No holds barred.

Was there any chance of them—all three of them—making a future together?

That, he believed, was where he'd gone wrong the last time around. They'd both known they should have waited to be together, and once it happened, he'd backed off. And so had she. So they didn't speak of it, and the gap increased between them until he hadn't known how to cross it.

He was the first to admit it would take a lot of work. The blunder he'd made with Matty and the goat was proof of that. But he was quickly learning that God was the God of second chances. And if the Lord opened up the door for him and Carolina, he was going to walk through it.

After the shake-up on Saturday, he'd gone to Sunday services at Haven's community church for the first time in his adult life. He hadn't known what to expect, but he'd actually enjoyed singing the hymns—however off-key he might have been—and Pastor Andrew's sermon about God's love and forgiveness only made Wyatt more determined than ever to straighten out his personal life.

He'd thought maybe people would judge him, as he'd never before seen fit to darken the door of a church, but everyone had been surprisingly welcoming. Pastor Andrew had even offered to meet Wyatt in private to answer any questions he might have about being a Christian.

He'd always envied Carolina's faith. It was amazing to realize the same God Carolina talked to so openly was willing to listen to him, as well.

His mind full of future plans, he showered and shaved and prepared for his usual Monday morning rounds. The beginning of the week was usually very quiet, and most of the local ranchers called his office if they needed to set up an appointment for veterinary services, so he was surprised when his cell phone rang.

Only in an emergency did anyone call his cell phone line. A cow that had suddenly fallen ill, or a mare in foal.

He glanced at the caller ID and saw that it was the number for the boys ranch.

"Wyatt?" It was Bea Brewster's voice on the line. "I think you need to get over here as soon as possible."

Wyatt could plainly hear the tightness in her voice, the near panic of her tone.

Bea Brewster never panicked.

"Is it one of the animals?" he asked, tucking the phone to his chin while he pulled on one tan cowboy boot and then the other.

"No." Bea swept in an audible gasp of air.

"Much worse. It's Johnny Drake. I knew you would want to know as soon as possible, since you mentor the boy."

"What about Johnny?" Wyatt's gut was churning like a combine. Johnny typically stayed in the trenches and avoided trouble. "Is he hurt?"

"No." Bea paused. "He's gone."

"What?" Wyatt's voice had risen an octave as his heart sprinted into gear. "What do you mean, *gone*?"

"His house parents went to find him when he didn't show up for breakfast this morning. He wasn't in his room. He didn't go to school. His duffel bag, most of his clothes and all of his books are missing."

"I'll be there in five," Wyatt said, even though the boys ranch was a good ten-minute drive away.

Panic seared his chest.

Why did it have to be Johnny?

What could have happened to the teenager that would press him to leave on the sly? Unlike many of the other boys, Johnny didn't have relatives waiting to pick him up when he was done with his time on the ranch. He was going to be aging out soon, on his eighteenth birthday—which, now that Wyatt thought about it, was coming up soon, at the beginning of April.

The ranch would allow him to finish out the

school year, but by then Johnny would have to make plans for what he was going to do next.

"Where are you, dude?" Wyatt said aloud, his voice echoing in the truck's cab.

He didn't know what prompted him to do so, but he used the Bluetooth on his dashboard to dial Carolina's cell phone number, which thankfully was on speed dial.

"Can you meet me at the boys ranch as soon as possible?"

"Wyatt? What's wrong? You sound as if you are about ready to jump out of your skin."

"I *feel* like I'm freaking out. I am about to have a major meltdown." He slammed his palm onto the steering wheel. "Johnny Drake has gone missing."

"*Missing* missing? Like he disappeared?"

"That's what Bea thinks. And I don't think he is coming back. He took his duffel bag with his clothes in it. Even more telling, he has all of his books with him."

"Oh, wow," she breathed. "Let me get Matty dressed and see if my next-door neighbor will watch him for a bit, and then I'll be right there."

Wyatt didn't know why having Carolina's presence at the ranch was so reassuring, but it was. He needed her support. He just hadn't realized until this moment how much.

Carolina's cabin was further from the boys

ranch than Wyatt's own ranch, so it was to his surprise she was waiting for him when he pulled up, already deep in conversation with Bea Brewster.

"Oh, Wyatt." Carolina's beautiful golden-brown eyes were glittering with tears. She murmured his name again and pressed herself into his embrace, wrapping her quivering arms around his waist and tucking her head onto his chest.

He held her tightly as a sense of foreboding washed over him. He couldn't tell by her tone whether she was seeking his comfort or giving hers, but holding her in his arms made it easier for him to get a grip on his emotions.

Carolina cared for Johnny. She had really gotten to know the teenager over the past few weeks. She had even had him babysit Matty on several occasions.

But she also knew how important Johnny was to Wyatt. The young man was far more than merely a kid he mentored. Johnny had given him purpose when he'd been floundering, had been a lifeline when he'd needed one. He had shown Wyatt that he could make a difference right where he was, without traveling to another continent to find meaning in his life. He was an indelible part of Wyatt's world.

So why would Johnny run away? Why hadn't he come to Wyatt first? He knew the boy was often the object of ridicule because of his stutter, but that had been the case all his life.

What had changed?

What would have caused him to take such a drastic action without letting anyone know about it?

Why had he run?

"Do you have any leads on him?" Wyatt asked, gently turning Carolina so they both faced Bea. He kept Carolina within the circle of his arms, her back solid against his chest. He wasn't going to apologize for it. He didn't care who saw his actions or how they interpreted them.

She needed him right now, and in the strangest way, he found relief for his own distress by offering her comfort, by being strong for both of them.

"We don't have a clue," said Bea. "He didn't tell anyone where he was going and he didn't leave a note."

"Maybe we're overreacting. When was the last time anyone saw him?" Wyatt ran a palm across his whiskered jaw.

"He was at dinner last evening. No one remembers seeing him afterward. He wasn't at any of the ranch's formal programs, but at the time, we didn't consider it any real cause for alarm. You know Johnny. Sometimes he gets his nose stuck in a book and forgets where he is and where he is supposed to be."

"I'm not trying to cast any kind of blame here, so please don't take this the wrong way," Carolina said with a catch in her voice. "But don't the house parents check the boys before lights-out every night?"

"Johnny's house parents, Eleanor and Edward Mack, did do a brief head count before lockdown last night."

"So then bedtime was actually the last time anyone saw him," Wyatt clarified.

"No. Unfortunately, Johnny played one of the oldest tricks in the books on us. He tucked a blanket inside his sheets to look like a body and left a hoodie propped on the pillow to create the shadow of a head. Ed didn't have any cause to take a closer look in the dark. He didn't suspect a thing. It was only this morning when Johnny didn't appear for breakfast that the Macks went back and discovered Johnny's duplicity."

As they spoke, several other folks arrived. News traveled fast in Haven. Some were employees and volunteers at the boys ranch, while others were members of the board of the Lone Star Cowboy League. Some of the older boys were also milling around, curious as to what had happened to one of their own.

Wyatt was grateful that he lived in the close-knit small town where residents looked after each other—and where folks counted the boys at the ranch in their number.

"We've got an additional problem," Bea continued, raising her voice so she could be heard by the growing crowd. "And it's a doozy."

A hush went over the people gathered in the yard.

"As most of you know, because of the recent thefts and arson, the Department of Family and Protective Services has been—" Bea paused, searching for the right words "—keeping a closer eye on us than they might otherwise be doing. And who can blame them? They have the boys' best interests at heart, just like we do."

Carolina's grip on Wyatt's forearm tightened and he laid his hand over hers. The gnawing in the pit of his stomach was turning into a sharp-toothed grind.

It didn't take a genius to figure out where Bea's concerns were taking her.

"We've had word that the DFPS is planning to make an unannounced visit soon—maybe as early as today. If they discover that one of our boys is missing—well, let's just say it will look bad for us. Of course, the most important thing is that we find Johnny and bring him back safe and sound. Then we'll deal with the authorities."

Gabe Everett stepped forward. "Okay, folks, it is obviously imperative, for both Johnny's sake and ours, that we locate the boy as soon as possible and return him to the ranch. We appreciate any help you all can give us."

There were several murmurs of agreement among the folks in the gathering.

"I think we should split into groups," Nick McGarrett suggested. "We can cover more ground that way."

"I agree," Bea said. "Gabe, Katie and I will stay in the office in case Johnny tries to make contact there, or the DFPS shows up. I will make a list of everyone's cell phone numbers and we will keep you all regularly updated via text message, so check your phones often."

"Nick and I will muster the house parents and double-check all the nooks and crannies in the main residence," Darcy Hill offered.

"Lana and I will cover the barns," Flint Rawlings added, joining hands with his fiancée.

Gabe assigned Tanner Barstow and Macy Swanson to the other outbuildings. Several members of the Lone Star Cowboy League stepped forward to offer to check on the ranch land, while a number of the town's residents planned to search in and around Haven. Pastor Andrew indicated that he would return to the church in case Johnny sought help there.

Wyatt and Carolina stood silently, still clinging together for mutual support.

Where would Johnny go?

Wyatt felt like he should know the answer to that question. He knew Johnny better than anyone else at the boys ranch. The answer fluttered in front of him like a butterfly, but when he reached for it, it eluded him, soaring just out of reach.

Carolina took his hand and led him away from the confusion of the still-forming search parties.

"What do you think?" she murmured for his ears only. "Do you have any idea where Johnny might have gone?"

Wyatt growled in frustration. "That's just it. I feel like I *do* know. I just can't quite put everything together in my mind. I've got to put this puzzle together. If I don't figure it out, I'll be the one at fault."

"Why?" Concern lined Carolina's voice and her hold on his hand tightened. "Do you think he might harm himself?"

Wyatt felt like a storm had descended over him. Clouds of black and gray settled on his shoulders, making it hard for him to think clearly.

"What? No. I mean—I don't think so. Johnny has been through a lot in his life, but he's got a solid head on his shoulders. He wouldn't do something stupid. I have no idea why he ran away, but I do think he believes he has a good reason."

"I don't understand. Why did you say you would be to blame, then?"

"I meant with the DFPS." He slid his hand from hers and grasped her shoulders, his eyes capturing hers. He needed to see that she understood what he was saying.

"Go ahead," she urged, giving him a moment to collect his thoughts and form coherent words.

"I'm not quite sure how to explain this to you, except to say that Johnny is my responsibility—my *personal* responsibility. I know he's currently a resident of the boys ranch, but our connection is special. It's more than just me being a volunteer, a teacher or even a mentor."

"You see a lot of yourself in him."

He framed her face with his hands and bent his head until their foreheads were touching. Her soft skin and unique floral scent somehow calmed his mind, and the feel of her warm breath against his cheek made his own respirations even out.

She understood.

More than that, she grounded him, kept him from drifting away in his anxiety.

She recognized his need to be the one to find Johnny. If anyone else got to the boy first, he would think he was in trouble, and then he would bolt away and disappear for good—if he hadn't already.

His heart clenched. Why did everyone and everything he loved always leave?

His parents, who had left him for foreign service and had never returned. His gran, whose mind no longer recognized his face. Carolina, who had vanished from his life once before, and he had no way of knowing whether or not she'd leave again—this time with the knowledge that she was taking Matty away from him as well.

Even the young buck he'd vetted ought to be out leaping through the waist-high Texas prairie grass, but instead was on the verge of leaving this world.

And now Johnny.

Wyatt concentrated, not on his own breathing, but on Carolina's. He lifted his mind and his heart in silent prayer, releasing all his pain and fear and allowing himself to be enveloped in the presence of God.

And then, as if the sun had finally broken through the clouds surrounding him, dissipating them into mist, his thoughts became clear, coherent and united.

Of course.

He smiled down at Carolina, but she couldn't see it because she had her eyes closed. Evidently she was praying, just as he had been.

Maybe God was answering both of their prayers. He could be wrong, but—

"Carolina, honey. I think I know where Johnny is."

Carolina trusted Wyatt's gut instinct, but she found it ironic that he suggested they return to his ranch. He'd come from there to meet with Bea and the others about Johnny's disappearance. Obviously he'd seen no trace of the teenager this morning.

Wyatt appeared deep in thought as they took his truck back to his ranch, and Carolina didn't want to disturb him. He was no doubt considering how he was going to handle the situation if Johnny was, as Wyatt suspected, somewhere on his property. It wasn't going to be an easy conversation.

Carolina was grateful it was Wyatt who had this lead and not someone else who didn't know Johnny as well. He was already going to be in a world of trouble when he was caught. He would need all of Wyatt and Carolina's help to run interference for him with the boys ranch.

Like Wyatt, Carolina had no doubt in her mind that Johnny believed he had good reasons for running away. She knew him to be a responsible young man who applied himself to his studies and his vetting work with Wyatt. She had no qualms whatsoever about leaving Johnny to babysit Matty.

She still didn't.

But she *was* worried about poor Johnny's current state of mind, and of course the impending DFPS visit to the boys ranch, which might have inadvertently been made worse by Johnny's sudden disappearance.

"I didn't get around to feeding the animals this morning," Wyatt said grimly as he pulled the truck to a stop in front of his ranch house and cut the engine. "Bea called me away before I had the chance. I think Johnny might be in the stable. He has always drawn comfort from being around animals."

"Do you want me to stay here so you can talk to him alone first?"

Wyatt's face held genuine surprise.

"What? No. I definitely think a little feminine compassion is called for here. Johnny really responds to you." He let out a breath. "Besides, I'm not even certain that my theory is correct. He could be halfway across the state by now, for all I know."

"Or he could be in your barn."

"Right." Wyatt pressed his lips into a hard line and gave a clipped nod. "Well, there's only one way to find out."

He exited the cab and went around to open her door, giving her a hand out of the truck. It wasn't that she really needed his assistance as much as emotional support. It was a nice gesture, especially when he closed his hand over hers as they set off toward the stable.

He paused just outside the door. "Let's hope I'm right about this."

She squeezed his hand in response. She immediately noticed one obvious difference when they entered the shadowed building—the sound of a pair of antlers butting repeatedly against a stall door.

"Wyatt, look!" She pressed forward, surprised to see the injured buck not only up on its feet again, but tossing its head and bleating in annoyance over being cooped up.

Wyatt's face was beaming as he approached the stall. "Well, now. Look at you. Easy does it, big fella."

"He's better?"

"I'd say so." Wyatt picked off his hat and slicked back his hair with the palm of his hand. "I can't believe my eyes. I really thought we were going to lose him."

As Carolina's eyes adjusted to the dimness of the interior of the barn, she noticed a brief movement in the back of the deer's stall, a scuttle toward the darkest corner.

"Wyatt," she said softly, nodding in the direction she'd seen the slight shadow of movement.

He arched his eyebrows and replaced his hat, then settled his hands on the stall door, ignoring the startled shifting of the buck.

"You can come out now, Johnny," Wyatt said,

his voice low, even and gentle. "It's just Carolina and me. No one else knows you're here."

There was a long moment of silence before Johnny unfolded his lanky frame from the back corner of the stall.

Wyatt opened the stall door and Carolina distracted the buck while Johnny slipped through and Wyatt clicked the lock back into place.

Now that Carolina could see Johnny was safe, she had to bite her lip to keep from chastising him. The relief that washed through her was quickly followed by dismay. He'd put himself in danger, not only by running away, but by crawling into the buck's stall the way he had. He might not have been intentionally trying to hurt himself, but spending the night in an enclosed space with a wild animal was hardly a wise thing to do.

She knew she would come off sounding critical, or worse yet, angry, so she held her tongue. Her emotions were all over the place, from the fear of not being able to find Johnny to the joy of once again seeing his unmanageable mop of curly hair. Anxiety, frustration and the realization of how much she cared for Johnny whirled together like a cyclone, creating a perfect storm she could barely contain.

"How long have you been here?" Wyatt didn't seem to be struggling with the same stresses she was feeling, or else he was better at hiding his emotions. But that was just as well. She'd let him deal with the fallout.

"I c-came here in the middle of the n-night," Johnny answered hesitantly, his stutter amplified by the direness of the situation.

"You bunked with a wild buck?"

Johnny nodded.

"Why would you do that? Haven't I taught you anything? You had to have known how dangerous that was."

"H-he was hurt. I thought he might be d-dying. H-he was lying on his s-side and was having trouble breathing. I p-put his head on my lap and stroked his n-neck so he would know he w-wasn't alone."

Carolina's eyes pricked with tears. Johnny had such a sensitive heart, and an enormous capacity for love. He reminded her of Wyatt in so many ways.

She only hoped this incident didn't ruin his future plans. She didn't know what doors needed to open in order for him to continue his education and training, but she hoped he would find his way. She well knew how difficult life could be for a young man in Johnny's position.

"I f-fell asleep. When I woke up, the buck was standing up. I think h-he's better now."

Wyatt's eyes left Johnny long enough to inspect the deer. "I agree. I'll need your help to return him to the wild where he belongs."

Johnny's enormous, thickly lashed brown eyes grew even bigger as he pushed that stubborn curl off his forehead.

"You're not m-mad at me?"

Wyatt's gaze flashed to Carolina before narrowing on the teenager. "What you did was wrong, but I think you already know that. There are a lot of people out looking for you right now, taking time out of their day to make sure you're safe."

"I'm s-sorry, sir."

Wyatt sighed. "I know you are. Listen. Why don't we stop by my kitchen and grab a cup of coffee before we take you back to the boys ranch? I'll text Bea to let her know we found you safe and sound and that she can call off the search."

Johnny squared his shoulders.

"I'm not going back."

Wyatt's hands briefly formed into fists. It was the first indication Carolina had seen of the frustration she knew that he had to be feeling.

"Johnny, this isn't up for discussion," Wyatt said firmly.

"You really gave us all a scare," Carolina added gently. "There are a lot of good people out there looking for you right now."

Johnny strode deeper into the stable and picked

up his duffel bag from behind a bale of hay, where he'd clearly hidden it the night before. The bag was overstuffed with books. Sharp corners were sticking out everywhere at odd angles.

Johnny struggled just to sling the thing over his shoulder. He wouldn't get very far dragging that much weight around with him.

"Let's at least talk about this," Carolina suggested, holding her hands out to show she meant no harm. It was like dealing with a wild animal. There was no telling what Johnny would do if he was pressed. The teenager was every bit as likely to bolt as the young buck in the stall behind them, if given the opportunity.

"I'm n-not going back," Johnny repeated, lifting his chin in open defiance. Carolina had never seen him behave this way—more like a rebel than the sweet boy who went out of his way to help injured animals.

Wyatt shoved his hands into the pockets of his fleece-lined jeans jacket and rocked back on the heels of his boots.

"All right," he said evenly. "Why don't you tell us why you left, and explain why you don't want to come back to the boys ranch with us. Are you being bullied? Is someone threatening you?"

Johnny's anxious gaze flitted from Wyatt to Carolina and then back to Wyatt again.

"We're listening," Carolina assured him softly. "We're not here to judge."

Johnny dropped his gaze and scuffed at the dirt floor with the toe of his boot.

"I am t-turning eighteen soon," he said miserably.

"Right," Wyatt agreed. "At the end of the school year in May you will age out of the program anyway. I don't understand. Why would you want to leave now? You're going to graduate from high school soon. You've worked far too hard to miss that."

"I d-didn't want to say goodbye."

Wyatt arched his eyebrows in surprise. "Why would you have to say goodbye? Aren't you planning to stay here in Haven? I'm sure I remember you mentioning how much you like the town."

"I d-don't have a family."

Carolina could feel Johnny's desolation as if it were her own. The sweet young man really was all alone in the world, and soon he would no longer be a member of the boys ranch, which was the only home he had.

Wyatt's head jerked as if someone had slapped him. He stepped forward and clasped the young man's shoulders, forcing him to meet his eyes.

"Yes, you do, Johnny," Wyatt said without a trace of doubt in his voice. "You do have a family, and a home—if you want it."

Carolina's heart clenched. Did that mean Wyatt was staying in Haven?

Wyatt was offering Johnny everything he'd ever wanted. A home. A family. She was genuinely happy for Johnny. It looked like there were some happy times coming for the boy, and no one deserved it more than Johnny. She didn't begrudge him any of it.

But it made her realize all that she didn't have, all that, until this moment, she hadn't even realized she wanted.

Why did it have to hurt so much?

Chapter Ten

❧

Johnny's words had hit Wyatt like a freight train. How could the boy not see how valued—how loved—he was?

"I would be honored if you would come live with me after you age out of the boys ranch program," Wyatt said, dipping his head so the teenager could see that his words were in earnest.

"W-why?"

"Well, for one thing, Haven and the boys ranch are keeping me really busy as a veterinarian. I was hoping maybe after you finished attending college and vet school that you would join my practice."

Johnny's eyes lit up like fireworks at the mention of school, but the flame was just as quickly extinguished, doused by the reality of the situation.

"I d-don't have money for school. I thought I'd h-have to learn a trade."

"You'll learn a trade," Wyatt agreed, clapping Johnny's back. "But you have to go to college to become a veterinarian. I have money. And there are scholarships available for a bright young man such as yourself. I'm sure you must have heard that the Lone Star Cowboy League offers a good one. I'll help you with the applications. Have you thought about which college you would like to attend?"

Johnny's mouth worked but no sound came out. He shook his head.

"No matter. We'll figure it out together. With your grades, I don't think you will have any problem being accepted wherever you apply. You may have to start spring semester, but we'll get you where you want to go."

Johnny's brows lowered over his dark, contemplative eyes. He looked far too solemn for a teenager.

Wyatt winked and smiled, trying to lighten the mood.

"W-why me?" Johnny choked out.

Why?

Wyatt had thought it would be obvious. Hadn't he already said?

Maybe not. He wasn't good with words. He hadn't meant to confuse the lad. It was important that Johnny knew exactly where he stood in Wyatt's heart.

"Because you are like a son to me."

A high-pitched squeal from beside him made him wince and he turned to find Carolina dabbing at the tears in her eyes, her breath coming in uneven hiccups.

"Don't mind me," she said between sobs. "I'm a sucker for happy endings."

Wyatt met Johnny's gaze and rolled his eyes. They both broke into laughter.

Women.

Something good happened and they cried. He offered her his handkerchief, which she took gratefully.

"D-does that mean M-Matty is my brother?"

"Of course it does," Wyatt affirmed. He grinned, knowing how much having a sibling—even one in name only—would mean to a young man who had, up until today, experienced a very solitary youth. After the aunt who had raised Johnny had died, he had no family to call his own.

"I want to officially adopt you. You'll not only be my apprentice, you'll be my son."

Johnny beamed.

"What about C-Carolina?"

Wyatt stiffened. He'd been completely unprepared for that question.

What *about* Carolina?

How did she fit into this picture? Was he finally ready to own up to the feelings he'd been tamping down since the moment she had returned to town with Matty in her arms?

He was still sifting through his thoughts and emotions when Carolina spoke.

"Oh, Johnny, honey, I'm afraid it doesn't work that way. You know how much we both care about you, but it isn't as easy as all that. Wyatt and I are Matty's parents, but we are not a couple."

Carolina's frank denial hit Wyatt like a punch in the gut. Every emotion that had ballooned to the surface now popped, as if she were throwing darts at them.

They weren't a couple.

Of course they weren't. He knew that. And yet...

She'd spoken the words softly but firmly, with little emotion in her tone.

He had to face the hard truth.

His feelings for her were all one-sided.

Again.

"B-but you wore red." Johnny stared at Carolina, his words faltering between bemusement and accusation.

It took Wyatt a moment to piece together what Johnny was saying, but he was faster than Carolina.

"The color of her blouse at the Valentine's social didn't mean anything, Johnny. It was only a coincidence."

"What was a—" Carolina started to ask, but Johnny interrupted her.

"But you d-danced together. I saw you."

"Wait. That letter was from you?" Carolina's expression was lined with surprise, and her voice held a note of astonishment. "*You* wrote that note? Not the mystery matchmakers?"

Johnny nodded, looking unhappy.

Wyatt felt bad for Johnny, but not as regretful as he did for himself. What a terrible time to realize that history was repeating itself.

He hadn't figured out how he felt about Carolina, so he'd never spoken of his feelings. And now it was too late for them. Just like last time.

"Johnny, you know why we danced together," Wyatt reminded him, and then quickly blew out a breath and backtracked. He hadn't meant to sound so harsh.

Carolina saved him from his blunder.

"Look, sweetie. I'm well aware Wyatt only danced with me to give you the courage to dance with Cassie. It's no big deal," Carolina assured him softly. "But you can't make more of it than it actually was."

"Besides, I'm sure Carolina will be around from time to time," Wyatt added.

He wasn't *sure* of anything. Carolina could be planning to up and move to Mars the day after the seventieth-anniversary party for all he knew.

Still, he hoped. Prayed. And he held his breath until she concurred.

"Yes, of course I'll be around." Carolina was addressing Johnny, not Wyatt, but that didn't stop relief from flooding through him at the affirmation in her words.

Where there was time, there was hope. Right? Or was he just kidding himself?

Until her next words stopped him short.

"At least until the party in March. After that we'll have to see where the Lord leads. I'm thinking about going back to school, myself, and I'm really excited about it. But Wyatt and I are parenting a child together," Carolina continued. "So at least for now, we'll be seeing a lot of each other. And if you don't mind, I would appreciate being able to call on you to babysit Matty once in a while. He really loves you, you know."

Johnny beamed. "I'd l-like that."

Wyatt's gut was grinding. What was she talking about? She was leaving Haven? Going back to school somewhere?

Did she want shared custody of Matty? He would take no less than that, and he wanted so much more. The thought made him sick. Matty should be raised by both his parents.

But now wasn't the time to hash out those details. He couldn't let his feelings for Carolina take over. Not yet. There were people waiting for them to return Johnny to the ranch.

"So can we head on back to the boys ranch then?" Wyatt asked, affectionately clapping Johnny on the shoulder and doing his best to smile.

Wyatt's heart was breaking, but Johnny's was just now starting to mend. For the moment, that would have to be enough for him.

"Everyone will be so glad to see that you're safe," Carolina said with a smile.

"I'm sorry for the t-trouble I've caused."

"It's no matter now," Wyatt assured him. "As they say, all's well that ends well."

Wyatt stole a look at Carolina, but she refused to meet his eyes.

Except when it doesn't.

Carolina struggled to keep her emotions in check as Wyatt pulled up to the boys ranch office. She had offered Johnny the front passenger's seat, but he was anxious about returning to the ranch and chose to sit in the back of the cab where he could be alone with his thoughts.

Obviously, she and Wyatt couldn't have any kind of serious conversation with Johnny in the truck, but then again, what was there to say?

Wyatt had made it crystal clear where they stood in their relationship, if she could even call it that. They were in a relationship insofar as parenting Matty was concerned, but that was as far as it went.

She didn't know why it was bothering her so much. Their status hadn't changed from this morning, before they had learned that Johnny had run away.

Everything was exactly the same. For the day. The week. And the whole last month, for that matter.

So what *had* changed?

As the realization of the truth washed over her, she clasped her hands in her lap so she had something to hold on to.

She had changed.

She was not the woman who had rushed out of Haven, pregnant and terrified and too proud to admit she couldn't do it all on her own—nor did she want to.

Wyatt was a fabulous father to Matty, just as she had known he would be. And now Wyatt's relationship with Johnny was blooming into fruition. She got choked up just thinking about what a wonderful life Wyatt had offered that young man. And having Johnny in his life would be a tremendous blessing to Wyatt, as well.

It was almost worse knowing that Wyatt intended to stay in Haven and not bound off to foreign lands. How could she ever have thought that he would put his personal dreams over a relationship with his son?

That wasn't who Wyatt was. It never had been.

Why had it taken her until now to realize that over the years, Wyatt's dreams might have changed? Since she'd been back, she had never once asked him about what he wanted out of life, but instead had made assumptions that she could now see were erroneous and maybe always had been.

It was as if her eyes were suddenly opened to the truth. Wyatt was happy living here in Haven, volunteering at the boys ranch and working as the town's veterinarian. And now he had a family to make it all worthwhile. Complete.

Except that family didn't include her.

Not really. Even though she now understood just how much she wanted to be a part of it.

Instead, she would be living on the outskirts of that family—on the outside of the house, looking in. Watching Wyatt and Johnny and Matty growing closer and closer as a family unit, while she would be all alone. Wyatt might eventually even marry, and—

She closed her eyes and willed away the thought. She couldn't even go there. Her pulse hammered in her temple. She didn't usually get headaches, but this one was almost more than she could bear.

Still, being distracted by a headache was better than thinking about her *heartache*.

"Looks like we made it just in time." Wyatt nodded toward the black SUV that had pulled up next to the truck.

A middle-aged woman, her blond hair clipped back in a tight bun, exited the vehicle. Not only was she unfamiliar to Carolina, but she had the clipboard-holding look of an official government employee stamped all over her.

"Am I in t-trouble?" Johnny's voice wavered with anxiety. He had seen the woman, too.

Carolina glanced back and smiled reassuringly. "I can't see why you would be. Once we explain the situation to Bea, I'm sure she'll understand."

"What about that l-lady?"

"I'll talk to her," Wyatt assured him.

An official-looking woman was shaking hands with Bea as Wyatt, Carolina and Johnny entered the front office. Gabe, Katie and Pastor Andrew were also present. Katie was seated at the desk with Pastor Andrew standing directly behind her. Gabe stood casually leaning his shoulder against one wall, his arms crossed in front of him.

Bea's eyes lit up with relief the moment her gaze landed on Johnny.

"You scared ten years off my life, young man, and I can't afford to lose that much time." Even as she was scolding Johnny, she was wrapping him in a big bear hug. "Wyatt, Carolina, this is Ms. Angela White from the DFPS."

Ms. White had an openly curious expression on her face but did not ask the obvious question.

Bea turned Johnny around by the shoulders and introduced him to the government agent.

"Johnny Drake here is one of our finest success stories. Before he came to the boys ranch, he was creating a bit of havoc in the school he was attending. He was probably just standing up to the bullies, if you ask me. Anyway, since he's been here, he has turned his life around. He's gone from flunking out of school to having straight A's, and he has been specially mentored by our veterinarian, Wyatt Harrow, who volunteers here at the ranch in his free time."

Bea gestured toward Wyatt, who tipped his hat in greeting but said nothing.

Ms. White's gaze moved from Wyatt to Bea and then finally settled on Johnny.

"Why do I feel like there is a part of this story that you are not telling me?"

Carolina's anxious gaze caught Wyatt's. Without saying a word, his eyes and expression bolstered her confidence.

"It was all a misunderstanding, really," Carolina explained. "You see, Johnny is aging out of the boys ranch program soon, and he no longer has any living relatives to go home to. He wasn't sure he could handle a formal dismissal, so he decided he would leave us early and avoid the agony of saying goodbye."

"He ran away," Ms. White summed up neatly, scribbling something on the memo pad on her clipboard.

"No," Carolina exclaimed. "Well, yes, technically, but as you can see, he's here now."

"Yes, I can see that." Ms. White drummed her pen against the clipboard and turned her speculative gaze on Johnny. "And what do you have to say for yourself, young man?"

"I d-didn't mean to cause any t-trouble."

Carolina inwardly cringed at poor Johnny's stutter, made more pronounced by his anxiety.

"I'm s-sorry I r-ran away. But I'm okay now. I have a new f-family. Right, Wyatt?"

Johnny's hopeful gaze shifted to Wyatt, who stepped forward and laid a hand on his shoulder.

"That's right. He'll be coming to live with me after the end of the school year. I'm going to make sure he gets into college and vet school, and then he will join me in my practice here in Haven."

"Why, that's wonderful," Bea exclaimed. "See, Ms. White? A real success story."

Carolina was all choked up by the way the drama was unfolding, and she had to blink back the tears in her eyes. She couldn't imagine that Ms. White didn't feel the same way.

"Let me speak frankly," said the agent. "There is no doubt that the boys ranch has done and is doing good things for the residents who participate in the program. I can even understand a little…slipup like Johnny's, although I expect I won't hear of any further incidents such as this one."

She paused and her gaze swept the room.

"My concern in coming here today is that you appear to have been targeted by a person or persons who wish to do the boys ranch—and possibly the residents who live here—harm. When innocuous pranks and petty theft turn to arson, the DFPS can't help but notice. I'm here to evaluate whether the boys' safety has been compromised."

"What does that mean for the ranch?" Gabe asked the question that was on everyone's minds.

"Well—Gabe, is it? What that means is that the boys ranch might need to be, temporarily, at least, suspended from providing services. We can't risk putting the boys' lives in danger. That is simply out of the question."

"I thoroughly agree," said Bea. "But I'm not convinced closing down the ranch is the best course of action. There must be some other way we can handle it."

"There is," said a deep voice from the doorway.

Carolina turned to see Texas Ranger Heath

Grayson taking up most of the doorway, none too gently shoving a man in handcuffs into the room before him.

"This is Donald Nall," Heath said grimly. "Bea, I think if you look up his name in the boys ranch records from about ten years ago or so, you will discover that his parents put in an application to have him sent here."

"Yeah, except you guys turned me down."

Nall lunged at Bea. Katie screamed. Carolina took an involuntary step backward.

It all happened in an instant, but Nall was quickly restrained again and never made contact with Bea. Heath had a good grip on his arm, and Wyatt and Gabe surrounded him. Standing about five-ten, Nall looked small compared to all the other men, and he didn't put up much of a fight.

Pastor Andrew drew Katie into his arms and smoothed her hair away from her face. "It's okay, sweetheart."

"This is all your fault," Nall accused basely, glaring at Bea. "You were supposed to fix me. You were supposed to *fix me*!"

Heath gave him a little shake. "Nall here has already done time on drug charges, and he has a history of mental health issues."

Bea nodded compassionately. "That was probably the reason why he didn't qualify for the boys ranch."

To Carolina's surprise, Bea stepped right in front of Nall and faced him squarely. "I am very sorry we were unable to assist you, Mr. Nall. Unfortunately, we have to turn down many worthy cases. I truly hope you will be able to find the help you need."

"Oh, he'll get the help he needs," Heath assured them. "He'll have plenty of time to do some soul-searching where he's going."

"Go with God's blessing," Pastor Andrew added. "We'll be praying for you."

"Are you serious?" Nall spat. "You keep away from me, preacher."

"Come on, Nall," Heath said as the sound of police sirens drew near. "Your ride is here."

Heath removed Nall from the room, and for a moment the only sound Carolina heard was the rasp of her own breath.

Bea turned to the DFPS agent. "So, Ms. White. Would you like a tour of the grounds? I can introduce you to some of the volunteers who work here."

The agent dropped the clipboard to her side. "I would really like that, but I think I will have to decline and make it another day. There is clearly no reason for me to tarry here, and I have a full caseload I need to address."

"Maybe you can come out some weekend when

you're free and take some time to look around," Katie suggested.

Ms. White showed her first real smile, and Carolina thought it brightened up her whole face. "I would like that. I'll show myself out now. You all have a great day."

A knock sounded just as Ms. White was leaving.

"Please come in," Bea told an unfamiliar woman. Pretty and young with short brown hair, the lady was accompanied by four-year-old twins.

"I'm sorry to bother you, but I'm looking for Bea Brewster."

"You've found her," Bea said with a smile.

"I'm Avery Culpepper?" Her voice rose as if it were a question and not a statement of fact.

"Avery Culpepper?" Gabe repeated.

Avery looked from one of them to the other. "I'm sorry. Are you all in the middle of something?"

"Not at all," Bea assured her. "You can't imagine how happy we are to see you. Have you checked into the hotel yet? I've got a bathroom next to my office where you can freshen up. I imagine you've had a long day of travel."

"No. I mean, no thank you. It has been a long day, and my girls, Dinah and Debbie, need to rest, but if you don't mind, I'd like to talk to you now. I'm not sure how long I'll be in town."

Bea smiled. "We'd like to persuade you to stay. Your grandfather left you an inheritance in his will."

"So I understand. I think it would help me to hear the details before I start considering my options." She blew out a nervous breath and smiled.

"Of course. Shall we go back to my office?" Bea gestured her through to the other room.

"Well," said Gabe, running a hand across his jaw, "that's two problems solved, anyway."

"You still haven't found your grandfather?" Carolina asked sympathetically.

"I haven't even had a single decent lead, and time is working against me." Gabe groaned and shoved his fingers through his hair.

"Is there anything we can do to help?" Wyatt asked.

"Honestly? I've got nothing."

Carolina cringed, because that was exactly how she was feeling, too.

She had nothing.

The group dispersed. Carolina was halfway to her car when Wyatt caught up with her, reaching for her elbow and whirling her around to face him.

"You're going back to school?" he demanded, his voice low and gravelly.

"I—yes. I'm thinking about it." She hesitated. She had put in applications to a couple of business schools and had been accepted, but she hadn't yet said anything to Wyatt. In hindsight, she realized she might have been putting the cart before the horse. Just because she wanted to stay in Haven and work in Wyatt's office didn't mean he wanted her there.

He certainly didn't look happy. He lowered his brow and clamped his jaw. "You would leave? With Matty?"

"Well, yes, but—"

"I'll fight you, you know. I didn't want it to come to this, but I won't let you take my son away from me. Not this time."

Was that what he thought she was doing?

She opened her mouth to explain and then closed it again as fury washed through her, followed by a new wave of guilt. Clearly Wyatt hadn't forgiven her for the past. He believed she was the same woman she'd been back then, a woman who would take his son away from him.

He might as well have stabbed her in the heart.

And he'd turned all her plans on end. If he didn't trust her, he wouldn't want her working for him, so attending school would mean nothing. She'd only planned to be gone for the few months it took to get a certificate in administrative assisting.

Which would be worthless, now. He had taken away her last lifeline.

In planning his own life—with Matty, and with Johnny—he'd taken away hers.

She would not leave Haven. She would not do that to Wyatt, not again, no matter what he thought of her. But as to the future?

An ocean of loneliness.

Chapter Eleven

It was a good day.

It was Gran's one hundredth birthday, and she not only recognized Wyatt, but even seemed happy to see him. Much of the town had gathered to help celebrate.

It remained to be seen whether this good day would become a great day, or else would degenerate into the worst day of his entire life. There was no middle ground here.

Sink or swim. Feast or famine.

But he had to know. He couldn't just keep on with the status quo. His life had to change, one way or the other. And today was the day he would make that happen.

"Queen for the day," Carolina said, approaching Gran with a sparkling silver tiara. "For the birthday girl. Don't you look just lovely?"

"Two prettiest ladies in the room," Wyatt admired, snapping some pictures with his cell phone. He laughed when Carolina hid her face behind her hands.

He was in awe of all she had done. She had planned and executed the whole party virtually on her own. She'd allowed Wyatt and Johnny in on her secrets only when it was time to decorate the main room at the nursing home.

All the crepe paper and banners were in various colors of green, since spring was Gran's favorite season. Accents were in sparkling silver and gold. The room really did look amazingly transformed. Carolina had spent hours making sure everything was just right.

They had invited most of the staff from the boys ranch, and many of the residents of the nursing home were milling around. Most of the elderly population had no idea it was Gran's one hundredth birthday, or even who Gran was, but they were up for a party.

And so, thankfully, was Gran. She was using a wheelchair today, but that didn't matter, since she was the center of attention. Matty, sporting a navy blue suit and a red bow tie, was entranced by the wheelchair and toddling around with Gran. She, in turn, was delighted by the boy.

"Are you ready to blow out the candles on your cake?" Carolina asked, wheeling Gran toward the table with a tiered cake. "Chocolate cake with chocolate frosting, just as you like it. We've even got chocolate ice cream."

Wyatt hushed the crowd and then led off a round of "Happy Birthday." Carolina chuckled at his off-key rendition and he laughed with her. He loved to see her happy.

He loved *her*.

Enough to let her go, if that was what she truly wanted. Once he'd calmed down from learning of Carolina's plans to go back to school, he'd realized she was a different person than the one who'd left him before. He didn't know anything for certain in this crazy world his life had turned into, but he trusted Carolina. She would let him be a part of Matty's life.

But he wanted so much more than that, and there was no time like the present to tell her so. He had an engagement ring—the one he'd purchased for her three years ago—burning a hole in his pocket.

Sink or swim was an understatement.

He found his moment and pulled Carolina aside.

"When are you planning on leaving?" he asked in a ragged whisper.

She straightened her shoulders and looked him straight in the eye. "I'm not."

"You should."

"I should?" Her eyes widened and color rushed

to her face. "Why? I mean, it's kind of pointless, isn't it?"

Wyatt felt like he'd lost track of the conversation. "I don't understand."

She shrugged. "All that matters is that I'm staying. So you can be with Matty." She didn't sound enthused about it.

He framed her face in his hands. "That's not all that matters, Carolina. If you need to go back to school to make yourself happy, then I want you to know I support you in that."

"You do?"

"Well, of course, if that's what you want. We've made a real success of coparenting that way."

She cringed when he mentioned coparenting.

"I had already decided to stay in town, even before you approached me just now."

Relief flooded through him, but he couldn't get past the niggling notion that something else was wrong.

"I found a business school where I can take all my classes online."

"You want to go into business?"

"I want to keep working for you."

"You do?" Now he was the one asking.

"That was always the plan. I was going to go back to school to become a certified medical office assistant. But I didn't speak to you about it first. How presumptuous of me. And I couldn't leave knowing I would disrupt your relationship with Matty."

Wyatt couldn't hold back his grin. She wasn't going to leave. It was *almost* the best news she could have given him.

So why didn't she look happy about it?

Maybe…just maybe…

His nerves were crackling and his heart was beating double time.

"The party is great. My gran is really happy."

She looked startled at the sudden change of topic, but after a moment she went with it. "I'm glad for her."

Wyatt caught Johnny's attention. The teenager was playing with Matty, and Wyatt motioned them both to join him, laughing and scooping Matty up into his arms.

"I've got to say, it looks like you've thought of just about everything where this party is concerned," he murmured close to Carolina's ear.

"Just about everything? What did I miss?" She cast her gaze around the room before her eyes returned to Wyatt.

Wyatt shoved his hand into his pocket and withdrew the diamond solitaire.

"This." His throat closed around the word.

Carolina's beautiful golden-brown eyes widened and her hand went to her neck. Matty grabbed for the shiny ring, but Wyatt laughed and held it out of his reach.

"This one is for your mama, big guy."

"I—you—"

"You're stuttering w-worse than m-me," Johnny teased.

"That's okay," Wyatt said, chuckling. Hoping. Praying. "All you have to say is yes."

"Yes," she whispered and held out her left hand so he could slide the ring on her finger. "But I thought—I thought—"

He laughed. "I can see that."

"You said we weren't a couple."

"No. *You* said we weren't a couple. And I'm fixing that little oversight right now. I realized after I had time to think about it that even if you were leaving town to return to school, you'd never leave me again. Not the way you did the first time. I trust you, Carolina. And I love you. It's not enough for us to coparent Matty. I want us to be a real family."

"I won't be on the outside looking in."

"No, sweetheart, you won't be," he assured her, his voice husky.

"C-can I call you Mom?" Johnny asked, his face turning a healthy shade of red.

Carolina kissed the teenager's cheek. "You'd better."

"Mama. Mama." Matty evidently felt he needed to add to the conversation.

"Your mama," Wyatt agreed enthusiastically. "My beloved wife."

Wow, that sounded good.

Her smile as big as the sun, Carolina wrapped one arm around Wyatt's waist and the other around Johnny's shoulder, forming a perfect circle.

A family unit.

Wyatt bent his head and softly kissed Carolina's lips, realizing his every dream had just come true.

Carolina's head was spinning. She couldn't help but flash the diamond solitaire, appreciating the glinting of the light off the cut of the stone.

This morning she had been alone, a coparent who would watch the love of her life move on with his, while she spent her heart-wrenching life alone.

Now she had Wyatt—and she had a family.
Thank You, God. Thank You, God.
She whispered the words over and over.

Katie approached and Carolina dropped her arm, but not before Katie had seen the ring. She squealed and reached for Carolina's hand.

"When did this happen? I'm so sure you didn't tell me."

Carolina laughed. "I only just learned about it a moment ago, myself."

"Wyatt just proposed?"

She nodded and put a finger over her lips. "Yes, but I don't want to make a big deal out of it. This is Gran's day. I don't want to steal her limelight."

"I'm sure she doesn't mind sharing," said Wyatt, coming up behind Carolina and wrapping his arm around her shoulders, drawing her close to him and kissing her on the cheek.

"Good thing, too. Because I see Bea headed our direction. Wyatt and Carolina are engaged," Katie spouted excitedly as Bea approached.

"I thought there might be something like that in the works," Bea said with a knowing grin. Carolina couldn't see how. *She* hadn't known anything was in the works until Wyatt had pulled that ring out of his pocket.

"Before I make a formal announcement," Bea continued, "I have another question for you, Carolina."

Carolina couldn't imagine how the day could get any better.

"I know you're working at Wyatt's office, but would you consider being a part-time nurse for the boys ranch? We can't pay as much as I imagine you were used to getting, and it's mostly going to be just scraped knees and bumped heads, but if you're willing, we'd love to have you."

Carolina couldn't speak. How could one day have gone from absolute misery to absolute bliss?

She nodded, and Wyatt gave her a reassuring squeeze.

"When God blesses, He really blesses," Wyatt murmured.

She turned toward him and lifted her face for a kiss. She was so wrapped up in Wyatt—the feel of his lips, the familiar scent of leather, animals and man that was distinctly Wyatt, his deep groan that sounded like a wildcat's purr—that she almost missed Bea's announcement.

Bea took her glass and tapped it with a spoon. "Ladies and gentlemen, I'd like to introduce the future Dr. and Mrs. Wyatt Harrow."

"Carolina Harrow," Wyatt murmured next to her ear. "That has a nice ring to it."

She turned into his embrace.

"I agree," she said between kisses that stole the breath from her. "And the sooner, the better."

* * * * *

If you liked this
LONE STAR COWBOY LEAGUE:
BOYS RANCH *novel,*
watch for the final book,
THE RANCHER'S TEXAS TWINS,
by Allie Pleiter, available March 2017.

And don't miss a single story in the
LONE STAR COWBOY LEAGUE:
BOYS RANCH *miniseries:*

Dear Reader,

Welcome to Haven, Texas, and the Lone Star Cowboy League's boys ranch! I'm so excited to have once again been asked to participate in a Love Inspired six-book continuity miniseries. I have enjoyed working with the other talented authors in this miniseries. It's been a great joy to add my characters to the workings of the boys ranch, the community of Haven, Texas, and a continuation of the Lone Star Cowboy League. If you're a new reader to Love Inspired continuity series, I hope you'll enjoy finding new-to-you authors who may become new favorites!

While the Lone Star Cowboy League and others connected to the boys ranch labor under the pressure of finding all the original members of the boys ranch before the seventieth-anniversary party as per Cyrus Culpepper's will, Wyatt Harrow and Carolina Mason are struggling with their own issues. Wyatt is shocked when Carolina returns to Haven after three years with a surprise he never expected—his two-year-old son, Matty. Trust and forgiveness are tenuous at best. Wyatt and Carolina have a long way to go to discover if, with God's help, they can learn to be a forever family.

I hope you enjoyed *The Doctor's Texas Baby* and the other books in this continuity series. I love to connect with you, my readers, in a personal way. You can look me up on my website at www.debkastnerbooks.com. Come join me on Facebook at www.Facebook.com/debkastnerbooks, or you can catch me on Twitter @debkastner.

Please know that you are daily in my prayers.

Love Courageously,

Deb Kastner

READERSERVICE.COM

Manage your account online!

- Review your order history
- Manage your payments
- Update your address

*We've designed the
Reader Service website
just for you.*

Enjoy all the features!

- Discover new series available to you, and read excerpts from any series.
- Respond to mailings and special monthly offers.
- Connect with favorite authors at the blog.
- Browse the Bonus Bucks catalog and online-only exculsives.
- Share your feedback.

Visit us at:

ReaderService.com

WESTERN WP PROMISES

YES! Please send me **The Western Promises Collection** in Larger Print. This collection begins with 3 FREE books and 2 FREE gifts (gifts valued at approx. $14.00 retail) in the first shipment, along with the other first 4 books from the collection! If I do not cancel, I will receive 8 monthly shipments until I have the entire 51-book Western Promises collection. I will receive 2 or 3 FREE books in each shipment and I will pay just $4.99 US/ $5.89 CDN for each of the other four books in each shipment, plus $2.99 for shipping and handling per shipment. *If I decide to keep the entire collection, I'll have paid for only 32 books, because 19 books are FREE! I understand that accepting the 3 free books and gifts places me under no obligation to buy anything. I can always return a shipment and cancel at any time. My free books and gifts are mine to keep no matter what I decide.

272 HCN 3070 472 HCN 3070

Name	(PLEASE PRINT)	
Address		Apt. #
City	State/Prov.	Zip/Postal Code

Signature (if under 18, a parent or guardian must sign)

Mail to the **Reader Service:**

IN U.S.A.: P.O. Box 1867, Buffalo, NY 14240-1867
IN CANADA: P.O. Box 609, Fort Erie, Ontario L2A 5X3

* Terms and prices subject to change without notice. Prices do not include applicable taxes. Sales tax applicable in N.Y. Canadian residents will be charged applicable taxes. This offer is limited to one order per household. All orders subject to approval. Credit or debit balances in a customer's account(s) may be offset by any other outstanding balance owed by or to the customer. Please allow 4 to 6 weeks for delivery. Offer available while quantities last. Offer not available to Quebec residents.

Your Privacy—The Reader Service is committed to protecting your privacy. Our Privacy Policy is available online at www.ReaderService.com or upon request from the Reader Service.

We make a portion of our mailing list available to reputable third parties that offer products we believe may interest you. If you prefer that we not exchange your name with third parties, or if you wish to clarify or modify your communication preferences, please visit us at www.ReaderService.com/consumerschoice or write to us at Reader Service Preference Service, P.O. Box 9062, Buffalo, NY 14240-9062. Include your complete name and address.

WPBPA16R